# BANJO GREASE

# BANJO GREASE

SELECTED STORIES

## DENNIS MUST

\* \* \*

RED HEN PRESS | *Pasadena, CA*

Book layout by Madi R. Foster

Library of Congress Cataloging-in-Publication Data

Names: Must, Dennis, author.
Title: Banjo grease : selected stories / Dennis Must.
Description: Second edition. | Pasadena, CA : Red Hen Press, 2019.
Identifiers: LCCN 2018059897 | ISBN 9781597090353 (tradepaper)
Classification: LCC PS3613.U845 A6 2019 | DDC 813/.6—dc23
LC record available at https://lccn.loc.gov/2018059897

The National Endowment for the Arts, the Los Angeles County Arts Commission, the Ahmanson Foundation, the Dwight Stuart Youth Fund, the
Max Factor Family Foundation, the Pasadena Tournament of Roses Foundation, the Pasadena Arts & Culture Commission and the City of Pasadena
Cultural Affairs Division, the City of Los Angeles Department of Cultural
Affairs, the Audrey & Sydney Irmas Charitable Foundation, the Kinder
Morgan Foundation, the Meta & George Rosenberg Foundation, the Al-
lergan Foundation, the Riordan Foundation, Amazon Literary Partnership,
and the Mara W. Breech Foundation partially support Red Hen Press.

Second Edition
Published by Red Hen Press
www.redhen.org

*For AVIVA*

# CONTENTS

# ESCAPE

**I**'D NEVER SLEPT with my father.

Until I went to Harvard. The closest I could get was its Divinity School where an interview had been scheduled with the Church History Department Chairman . . . the designated judge. To that point I'd passed through all its admission chambers.

Neither Father nor I had ever been to Boston. He dropped out of school in the eighth grade, Mother in the fifth. She thought my going to college in the first place was ill-advised. "It's something sons of doctors and businessmen do," she said. "Your father has been hanging around drinking with too many of them."

He had been, in fact. And the day I received an offer of a scholarship to a small all-male college a few hundred miles south of Hebron, Father began picking out my wardrobe. Mother called him a fool, and chastised me for indulging him.

"Why should you be any different than the rest of us? Now it's your turn to bring money into the house."

Like most of my relatives, Father was employed by Neshannock, a large plant on the banks of the river of the same name that manufactured chinaware for hotels, restaurants and diners across the States. The family chain of Daugherty and Coleridge potters hadn't been broken for two generations and now I, bolstered by his encouragement, was threatening to break the covenant . . . to Mother as sacred as attending church each Sabbath.

Not until much later in life did I understand that I was his surrogate for "getting out." If I could escape Hebron's suffocating fate, then he, albeit vicariously, would, too. And on this issue he stood right up to her.

"He's going."

I'd been programmed for working for Neshanock and raising a family in Hebron. Furthermore, all my friends were staying back. "It's something the snobs on the hill do, not you, for Chrissake, Daugherty. Who's gonna help us keep the cooz happy?" Mother had all the evidence on her side. But Pap'd already taken me to Levine's Men's Store to purchase that "college" suit, a double-breasted blue serge. Even a felt hat (which I never wore) and a pair of black, cap-toed banker's shoes.

"You look like Tom Flaherty," he crowed as I stepped out of the dressing room. "Abe, doesn't he look good?"

"This damn burg is dead," Abe replied. "There's got to be a better way. Your old man is right. Get the hell out while you can. You'll find a better woman, too. The smart ones want an educated man—not some pasty face smelling of red Neshanock clay." He smiled ruefully at Father.

When I stepped out of Abe's store that morning, his window displayed one bone-colored mannequin wearing my suit with a price tag the size of a convict's number. I could see myself after ten years at the pottery, or even the bronze foundry, stooped over and bleary-eyed like the rest of the Hebron citizenry. Also, each day it was becoming harder to turn back; Pap insisted on parading me before all his working-stiff buddies at the Diamond Cafe.

"My son Westley's goin' off to Grant and Lincoln on a full scholarship!"

Raw approval in their glances. It wasn't another ribald tale Joe Daugherty was passing off. Gossip about the plant. The line that week on the Steelers. His boy was going off to college. Just like the sons of those swells on the Hebron's North Hill. *Sonofabitch!*

As if I were escaping. They kept patting me on the back . . . Chrissake, as if I were their son. Pap put away three boilermakers; I'd agreed to down one shot of bourbon. *"It's what educated people drink.*" Once outside, the sun near blinded us, for the beer joint was darker than the Greyhound bus depot, lit only by neon "Duquesne Pilsener Beer" signs in red and blue blinking above the mirrored bar.

"Where to now?" Pap asked.

"Well, I need a toothbrush and some toothpaste," I said.

"Oh, personals!" he gushed. And guided me into Eckard's drug store, two up from the saloon.

"Sal, my son Westley, here, is going off to college. He needs a toothbrush and toothpaste. What do the college people use?" The pharmacist showed me some arcane magma that cost twice as much as the regular, and handed it to Father as if he were giving him a fiver. "It's the good stuff, Joe. Flaherty buys a new tube each month." (Flaherty owned the bronze factory and lived in a Tudor mansion on the hill.) Pap proudly handed me the paste.

"Not that I give a shit," he said when we stepped outside, "but all these years I ain't ever known this tusk-scrub existed. Your mother and me been using Arm & Hammer. But Tom Flaherty and his silk-stockings did. The secrets of the rich . . . *sonofabitch!* That's why you're going off to school, kid. The bastards intend to keep us in the dark to perpetuity."

And when Mother smelled booze on both our greetings, she blanched.

When I returned home the following summer, just when she'd begun to niggardly warm up to the fact that I was, indeed, going to continue my studies, I told her God's existence might be a hoax.

"What are you talking about?" she cried.

"Well, Mother, I learned in philosophy class that God may be nothing more than a figment of your imagination." Our kitchen sat funereal dark that evening. I heard her crying to him behind their bedroom door later: "First you turn him into a North-side swell. Then you make him an atheist. What's your next trick, Joseph? . . . You and your highfalutin' ideas."

\* \* \*

Four years later, after receiving my degree in philosophy, I headed back home, sat down at the kitchen table, and announced to them both I intended to become a preacher. Father had no problem with my calling. If I wanted to climb up into a pulpit every Sunday morning to cajole sinners, that was fine with him. The pottery had bleached away all his juices but didn't own me.

Mother phoned her sisters. "Westley's going to Harvard to study to become a preacher. Will wonders ever cease?" The women of Hebron adored their preachers—the most loved men in town.

When I asked Pap if he wanted to take a trip with me to see the Harvard historian, he happily agreed to take a couple days off from work. So the first week in December we drove out of town in my 1952 Ford Fairlane . . . a decade-old, flamingo and cream oil burner. We decided to conserve what little money we had for "restaurant" meals and a bar tab instead of wasting it on motels.

The longest haul was across the entire length of the Pennsylvania turnpike. We encountered mostly a mixture of sleeting rain and gusting winds. Numbing iron-gray skies with umber fields on either side of us. The heater fan in the Ford pinged as if it were nicking Pap's bluchers. We talked most of the trip—even when one of us was supposed to be sleeping. Just outside Scranton—it was close to 10 p.m. now—when it became his turn again at the wheel, I glanced over and saw that he'd dozed off. I exited the turnpike and spotted what looked like a budget-rate motel . . . one still managed by its owner, who slept in the room behind an all-night office.

"What's going on?" Pap woke with a start when I pulled into the gravel lot.

"Twenty dollars isn't going to break us. I got to be fresh for the interview tomorrow."

Appointed with plastic Irish-lace curtains, puce chenille bedspreads, a mustard-yellow carpet, and one broken-down Danish modern chair alongside twin beds . . . our room was stone-cold. A toilet and a severely rusted metal shower stall sat off in a closet. But there were clean towels and a fresh roll of toilet paper. An electric heater, installed in the wall between the beds, I turned up full throttle. We each undressed and, wincing, crawled under the covers.

"Wait before you turn out the light," Pap said. The switch for the overhead light was above my headboard. He proffered a pint of Seagram's from under his pillow. "It'll help warm you up," he said. "These places ain't for road-weary folk like you and me, Westley— you especially, heading off to preacher's school. It's a poontang stop. Short on the amenities."

"But, Pap, it was only twenty dollars."

"I'm a cheap date." He laughed.

Sometime during the night I was awakened by a thundering in the bathroom. I got out of bed. The motel's exterior corona illuminated Pap—naked, pissing what sounded like pellets of hail into the shower stall.

"What in God's name are you doing?"

"What's it look like?"

"But the toilet's behind you!"

"This way I won't dribble on the floor," he said. "Worse things have happened in a notcherie, boy."

I lifted the bottle from under his pillow. Empty.

\* \* \*

Once we had crossed the Massachusetts line, we assumed we could drive straight to the university; that there would be signs saying Harvard. When we finally got to Cambridge and parked near the Yard, it was equally near impossible to find its Divinity School.

"A theology school at Harvard?" Passersby shook their heads in disbelief.

Pap said he wanted to stay in the car. Quartered in a Gothic building with turrets and stained-glass windows, the seminary sat amidst a stand of century-old oaks. A black-garbed ascetic (his severe manners and gold-rimmed glasses recalled Arthur Dimmesdale) greeted me in an empty classroom across whose chalkboards snaked the graffiti *Agape*. The interview did not go well at all. Five minutes into it I knew Pap and I would never boast about my going to this university.

The historian insisted on facts. *"The mission of the Church predicated upon Her illustrious history—what is your understanding of it, Mr. Daugherty? We are scholars here, sir, more than we are impassioned believers.* (Holy Rollers?) *Which I suspect you are inclined to be. We proselytize, not by emotion, but by the sheer weight of the Bride of Christ's edifice, her esteemed tradition and lucid rationale."*

He kept fingering his watch fob. I knew I was dead, and felt pretty glum about having dragged my father all the way to Boston.

"They didn't like you, eh Son?"

"I spoke in a Marlon Brando vernacular, he said."

"Uh-huh," Pap groused. Like he'd expected it.

"I wasn't erudite enough."

"What the hell's that got to do with spreading the gospel?"

"He grilled me on transcendentalism and the Reformation, spoke Latin phrases to me—archly amused by it all. It was awful. I thought he was going to put my sincerity to the test."

"That Christ died for our sins, right?"

"Something like that."

He spat. "This goddamn town of scholarly swells . . . I been sitting here watching them all bounce into their fancy towers of learning. See them walking on the balls of their feet? Drop your head between your knees and kiss your ass goodbye, Westley, if you think for one minute you're answering God's calling by enrolling here. Harvard Divinity School . . . *Hosannah Horseshit!*

"Maybe to make money. Or write books Jesus H. Christ himself couldn't decipher. And say they *did* accept you, Son?" He jabbed the buttons on the mute car radio. "Three years later you come back to a dink town like Hebron. Who's gonna listen to you? *And even if they did, who'd understand? We're in the wrong country, boy. These are not our people."*

He was right, of course. I wanted to matriculate not because of God, but because of Harvard. As if I were about expunging my past. And there it was sitting waiting in the car for me—smoking filter-tip Kools. *Now's the time, Son, to turn and face me, embrace me, accept your past, love it, be proud of it, then make something of it. Not expunge it.*

Maybe he was telling me he didn't want to be erased, too. Left behind while I roamed for three years inside that crenellated Gothic battlement to exit a stranger of God. And Pap'd wave to me from the cloudy interior of my old Ford. Our secret hand signal that we dreamt up when I was a kid (in unfamiliar or strange circumstances, he'd mirror it so that I never felt abandoned)—*but now I wasn't responding*, and he's tapping on the window with our spare change.

So it was his way of embracing his growing son this raw morning in Cambridge. Yes, he'd pissed in the shower stall the night before . . . like other fools. But this was the real Joe Daugherty speaking to me in *men's* language.

*Don't go out there too far, Son. I mightn't be able to save you. I ain't that strong a swimmer, you know.* That's what Pap was telling me.

The Cambridge lingo inside those battlements—he couldn't comprehend it. If I entered and came out in three years, we might become estranged. How fathers sometimes have to speak to sons? Maybe he'd finally seen the absurdity of that *beau monde* blue serge. Figured, too, that God didn't exist, then after a couple of years thought better of it—when time came racing forward. So our trip to Harvard . . . well, it was on the cheap. Even if old bitter-cup Dimmesdale had drawn a dripping red X through my application.

He'd saved me. And Pap, too.

\* \* \*

It was bone-chilling cold outside, and Father wanted to get back on the turnpike, head home. For the first few hours it was quiet in the car. Both of us staring up ahead. The expectation is always the greatest part of any adventure, it seems. Of course my pride was hurt. *What if I had been accepted?* He'd have put up a good front . . . but we were traveling buddies now. Nothing had come between us. Very little that I didn't know about him. Likewise, he me.

Then the snow started to come down in great sheets and within one-half hour the driving on the turnpike became treacherous.

Soon it would be dark. Cars up ahead of us began to skate off the road down the embankment. I slowed the Ford to fifteen miles an hour and knew we had to exit as soon as possible. The snow wasn't stopping and he and I could become stranded; our gas tank was running low and I couldn't keep the heater going for long. Father had begun to cough. Periodically when I'd glance over at him, I noticed he clutched the door handle and mechanically pumped his right foot against a ghost brake pedal.

We heard ambulance sirens behind us. Far behind us. The wipers' fan-shaped arcs on the windshield narrowed like eyes. We watched the car immediately in front of us—our lead—fishtail, accelerate into a dizzying whine, then plummet its occupants into a deep ravine. Father turned white.

"We have to stop," he said. "We ain't going to make it."

I thought so, too. But if we did stop, I was afraid he might succumb, for I noticed he was much older now. He'd been sick with a bad heart when I was away at school. The cough was more persistent. And the blizzard gave no sign of let-up. We could have been stranded for days. Surely he would perish.

"A turn-off is coming soon. I know it. We'll creep off and find a place to stay."

"How soon?"

"Soon," I said. "It's just up the road a way."

Darkness fell. No cars were passing us. Several had stopped dead in the highway, carcasses mantled in snow. I crept around them, uncertain how far ahead the exit road was. I had no idea, but had to make him believe. The bitter chill inside the car mocked the heater's lilting chatter . . . and Pap reeked of vulnerability. It was a *father-sweat* only a son can detect. *Son-sweat* he had smelled numerous times. Calling him into my boyhood room at night. Or when he snatched me out of a Lake Erie undertow, and pumped air into my chest. I was wet with the lake then, the sea-green lake, but he could smell my sweat. It rose up into his red nostrils that dilated like an animal's as he beat life back into me, crying for me to return. And, years later, he smelled my sweat the night my wife left me and I, foul of urine, called him from a phone booth in a strange

DENNIS MUST • 17

town at three in the morning, crying my guts out that I didn't know what I was going to do. That my life was over and I couldn't stop myself from caterwauling while racing across bridges, teasing the car against guard rails at seventy miles an hour. "WHAT AM I SUPPOSED TO DO, PAP?" I cried over the phone lines. And even though we were hundreds of miles apart, he smelled blood-sweat that night, a pungent ringing over those rural phone lines. He tried to calm me down. To breathe oxygen back into my heart again. To keep it from tearing itself apart over *a woman, a woman, a woman* . . . that sounded like another cry, another way to wail to me. But he knew about women, too, and blew peace back into my heart. And I began to breathe easier, slowing the Mercury down, promising him I'd come home to talk to him before I did anything drastic. The gamey, sulfurous odor of my sweat became more pleasant over the phone lines.

But now I smelled his. Big time. He was hunched up in the corner of the front seat, holding onto the chromium door handle, as if we were in an airplane, a single engine one, he—Lindbergh and I, out over the Atlantic, and he was the ghost and I was the ghost's son and we were trying to do the impossible—the ghost didn't want to die again. Goddamn NO. And the sweat inside the cockpit was stronger than woman odor, the odor of sex to which we were both addicted. It focused us, just like the odor of sex, woman-leg breath. We were high on it and scared to death. Neither of us talking. I'm taking the slippery-slope-to-Hell turnpike at five miles an hour now . . . faster than God's sleight of hand . . . looking for an opening, a pathway off, a little village with lights at the bottoms of all these fucking mountains, these Alleghenies . . . and him crying . . . *"Do you see it yet? Is it up ahead? Westley, can you see it?"* And me lying to my father like I ain't ever done before . . . *"It's right ahead, Pap."* And him answering, *"But you keep saying that. It's right ahead. It's right ahead."*

And that was our mantra. *"Keep saying it, Pap. Don't stop saying it. It's right ahead. By God if Jesus is with us . . . maybe he'll look kindly on us for forsaking Harvard today"* . . . and amidst *his* sweat

I could smell his gallows smile. Lime quick. But then it got real serious again.

"Are we gonna die on the Pennsylvania Turnpike, Westley, for Chrissake?"

We might've. Crossed it enough times in our lives. Sure seemed appropriate. But what an unforgiving death it would be. He was coughing continuously now. I was being challenged to bring the fucking airplane in. Playing the father's role now. I ain't ever been in that seat before. And with him alongside me, incapacitated. My real chance at being the old man, the Pap of this man-marriage, this godly companionship who believed in each other's myths, never caring whether they were true or not. I could see his lights in me, he could see mine in his. All we need to guide us through the night. Our stars in heaven, probably as close to it as we'd ever get. My star in his. His in mine.

That's what I had to guide me that night, and carefully I crept down the mountainous exit ramp, steeper than a coal chute it seemed, so easily we could have skied right off its flimsy parapets, tumbled to our certain deaths hundreds of feet below. But we didn't, and even the *lighted* toll booth had been abandoned as we crawled onto the main road. One motel outlined in yellow neon was the only corona in sight.

Each of its occupancies had a car parked out in front. Father was sick now. He was shivering. The booze was gone. He wasn't about to wait in the car. "What choice do we have?"

"We're full up," the attendant said.

"We'll take whatever you have," Father pleaded. "Anything. I'll pay to sleep in your cellar if you have one. We'll freeze to death in that car."

The man thought. If it had been just me, the *no* would have been firm.

"Well, I do got an unfinished attic. It's cold as hell up there, but I can give you plenty of blankets and furnish you with this little heater here I use to keep my legs warm."

"We'll take it," Pap said. And handed the man twenty dollars. "What do you got to eat?"

"Nothing except those candy bars in that machine over there."

Pap went over and fed all his coins into the vending machine. Six Hershey bars, a Baby Ruth and one Butterfinger. He cleaned out the machine. We followed the man and his flashlight into the attic. Just like he said. We could see the rafters and had to watch out for head-knockers. The man piled six blankets onto the bed and jury-rigged the coil heater to working. There was no bed lamp or toilet. He set a milk pail next to the window. And to think we almost got into Harvard that morning. Pap and I took turns pissing into the pail, then crawled into the bed with all our clothes on and started our candy-bar dinner. He liked the Hersheys. Ate every damn one of them. First time I'd seen him eat a candy bar.

He was breathing easier now. The coughing spasms had quieted down, too. Farther apart now. And that *fear-sweat*—I could detect it no longer. Almost as if we were home. In the orange glow of the heater's coil I felt the rhythm of his breathing struggling to get in tune with mine. A kind of father-and-son harmony. It was peaceful in that attic room. I knew he was fully awake, just as I was. We were lying there in the solitude of a strange country place off a perilous highway not thinking about sleep. Now we were cataloguing the day that had begun with a visit to a church historian in Cambridge, then wound treacherously back toward Hebron. And mutely I was thanking him for being with me and he, I know, was grateful that I drove. Where he might not have been able to.

But he did drive me out of Cambridge, he did by God drive me back home, and he did by God fall asleep in my arms; by God he did.

# CHRYSALIS

M Y MOTHER HAD two sisters, Christina and Lorraine. We lived on the east side of Hebron, they on the south side. The east side had many churches, the south side few. But they did have road houses and ethnic clubs, or "halls," where dances were held Friday and Saturday nights. I knew my aunts by name only, uttered when my father wished to cast aspersions on Mother's family. If I inquired about her mysterious sisters, Mother'd refuse to answer. Father would say they were in business.

"What kind of business?"

"They peddle fish," he'd guffaw, and Mother would leave the room.

He had a sister and a brother whom I also never saw. Uncle Mark traveled the States with the Mills Brothers Circus. Father said he was a lion tamer. To which Mother would retort: "And a whoremaster."

Agnes, his sister, even my friends knew, danced on stage Saturday evenings at the local BPOE. The family seldom talked about her either.

So when birthdays, Thanksgivings and Christmases were celebrated, it was just the three of us. No cards or gifts or even trips to the homes of my uncles and aunts. I found it very peculiar, inasmuch as I thought that's what relatives were for. Places to visit and get presents from. Also, I knew there were cousins whom I'd never met.

But it was Christina for whom Mother held a soft spot. Father clearly had dismissed his siblings, even to the point of crossing the street when either of them approached. And Lorraine, well, she lived in a cellar with a tar-paper roof (she was saving money, ostensibly to build a house on top of it), and stole meat from the local A&P. While Christina, Mother said, lived in a fine white brick home in the hollow with some Polish gentleman and drove a new Mercury sedan.

We clearly didn't have the kind of money she did. Father's car was twenty years old and periodically I'd paint whitewalls on its tires before he'd go out on a summer evening. Mother was an avid churchgoer and the only time she dressed up fancy (an iris dress and black cloth coat with buttons as large as silver dollars) was on Sundays for morning service and then again at vespers. Father dressed fancy Friday and Saturday nights to return early the next morning, stumbling drunk up over the banks of our front yard.

Even at that early age, I'd detected a puzzling incongruity operating between them. Mother, a pious woman who seldom wore makeup and prohibited foul language or alcohol in the house, kept our bungalow, its sparse furniture, and her person pathologically clean. She and the house smelled of Clorox, Lysol or Oxydol. Father, on the other hand, who fancied himself a forties Lothario, had an easy laugh. When he spoke warmly about Mother, it was only in the context of what an "extraordinary mother" she was, and that she'd missed her calling: "She should've run an orphanage."

For years I thought that was a compliment. Until adolescence when I understood it was an additional way to wound her. Like he'd shame her by bringing up Christina or Lorraine's names. And herein lay the incongruity.

It had been cloaked in childhood ignorance. A conundrum that nagged at me but resisted clarification. (Early on I had seen the word "sex" printed in the Sunday paper. I asked her what the word meant. She replied that it was a word I wasn't to use.) On Saturday or Sunday morning, if I happened to be up before the two of them, I might glance into their bedroom. I'd see Father naked, lying askew with the cover off him, his arms akimbo, as if he'd thrashed through the night and was utterly spent, and Mother primly "mummied" up on the edge of the mattress, stiff and wound tight in a blanket. The face of the incongruity.

But what mystified me then was Father's two seemingly contradictory taunts to Mother. I soon understood the *she-should-never've-gotten-married* dagger. *Her talents as a mother are beyond reproach.* I'd kind of liked him until I understood what he really meant. It did hurt her. Often when he went out on Friday and Saturday nights, she lay up in the bedroom crying. Her telling me "sex" was a dirty word, and now understanding that *he* thought it was the spring in a windup mouse. A secret even bigger than Santa Claus that didn't turn out to be a lie. As if she'd been born missing a leg or an eye, swindled him into believing she was a "woman" when it turned out she wasn't . . . only a mother. I began to hate him for this rancor towards her. His belittling her feminine attributes.

That was on the one hand. On the other . . . his causing her humiliation by bringing up the names of her sisters, Christina and Lorraine, in a derisive manner, my mysterious aunts—well, what the devil was that all about? He laments he married a mother and not a courtesan, but then castigates her because her sisters might be ones? I just didn't get it. I don't think Mother did either.

Until I came home from school one fall day and found a note on the kitchen table.

"I've left your father," it said. "I discovered he's been seeing other women. When he goes out to play poker on Friday and Saturday nights? Well, maybe he does, but now I know he sees women, too. And in particular one woman—Ethel James. (She was my mother's best friend whom I considered my surrogate "aunt.")

"Westley, ask him what the phrase *'Til Death Do Us Part* means.

"You take care, Son. Once I get settled somewhere I'll call you. Be a good boy. Love, Mom."

When Father came home that evening, I handed him the note and it was the first time I saw him lose heart.

"What are we going to do?" I said.

"I don't damn well know."

"Who's going to cook?" I asked.

"Me and you, I guess."

"Who's going to wash our clothes?" I asked.

"Same," he said.

"Is she ever gonna come back?"

He shrugged, sat down at the kitchen table, lit a cigarette and stared out the kitchen door over the back yard. It was muddy out there and bleak. The house felt cold and dark. After a while he said,

"Whadaya want to eat?"

"I don't know. How 'bout you?"

"You like sardines?"

"Fish?" I said.

"Little ones in mustard. They make good sandwiches."

"I ain't ever tried them," I said.

"Well, let's pretend you and me just went fishing and we pulled these out of Pymatuning Lake (a big one 100 miles from Hebron; we never went there). And you can make the Kool-Aid."

So I pulled out a loaf of Wonder Bread and we didn't even put a tablecloth on the Formica-and-chrome table. He slathered one piece of bread with yellow stadium mustard and opened the tin of sardines that I didn't even know we had. Laid four headless ones out on my mustard bread and on his, then covered them over with a clean white slice. And he cut them in two with a butter knife. Oil and mustard began to bleed up through the white bread and out onto the grey spackled Formica. I poured two large glasses of cherry Kool-Aid and we sat across from each other eating quietly. Kind of like friends. And he smoked.

We did this for five nights straight. It was on a Monday Mother left us. Friday night he didn't go out. Read the *Hebron News* in the living room after dinner, then went to early bed. On Saturday after work, he came home and said maybe we should change our menu.

I agreed. Though I had grown to like the sardines, especially when on the third night he cut up some onions on them. It helped cut the oily taste that lingered long after dinner was over. So I said, "Well, what can we eat now?"

"Eggs," he said. "Saturday night is a good egg-supper night. Go down to the corner store and buy a dozen. And get another loaf of bread. We got plenty of margarine she left us, and buy some more Kool-Aid. Any color you want."

When I returned home with the groceries, Pap had made up the table real nice. He had dressed it with Mother's hand-embroidered tablecloth, the one she used for Sunday meals. He even had napkins under the silverware and placed a knife inside the spoon on the right side and a fork on the left-hand side of the plate like Mother had always done it. (I still hadn't heard from her; had no idea where she was.)

"We like them scrambled," he said. I thought it was OK, and he began breaking the eggs into a black iron skillet, two at a time until he had the whole dozen bubbling almost to its rim. He poured in a lot of pepper and salt. And asked me to hand him the ketchup.

"What's that for?" I asked.

"Hell," he answered. "We put it on em after; why can't we do it while they're cookin'? Gives em color, too," he boasted.

That's when I noticed he was wearing Mother's apron. And when the eggs were ready, he proudly spooned them onto our plates as if he'd done something real special. He stood over me as I took a fork-full . . . seeing if they were done to perfection. But the toast had begun to burn, and he dropped the plate of eggs before me and rushed over to the toaster like I'd seen her do on Saturday or Sunday morning.

Soon we were both sitting across from each other again, and it was real pleasant, him and me, eating eggs with red veins in them. Then we doused them with even more ketchup and watched the margarine melt into the toast. We drank grape Kool-Aid . . . and both were real quiet and enjoying our meal . . . when halfway through he looked up and said:

"You heard from your mother?"

I said I hadn't.

"Oh," he said.

"You seen her?" I asked.

He didn't raise his head, but shook it. The moths were beating against our screen door. I told him I'd wash the dishes that night and clean up the kitchen. He seemed appreciative and went in and read the paper. We both retired early. And that's the way it went for nearly three months. Sardine sandwiches through the week. Eggs and toast on Saturday evening. Sunday evenings he took me to Coney Island Lunch where we each had buttermilk and two chili dogs with everything on and then went to a movie at the old Paramount Theater. There was always a double feature there and since it was war time, most of the movies were about Nazis.

I was glad I was seeing them flicks with him. Sometimes the Nazis did terrible things to the women in the pictures. If I'd have seen them with Mother, it would have unsettled me more. But with Pap and me riding back in the dark to our empty house, I kind of felt better about it all. He was my father and I wasn't afraid they were going to come and take him away. Whereas they might've stabbed Mother with her scissors.

Father ceased going out alone at all. And as far as I could tell he didn't touch a drop of liquor. He came home from work promptly each night and there were never any mysterious phone calls from women. It was almost as if we were camping out. I'd watched and helped Mother wash clothes long enough that I knew how to do it. So, just like she did, Mondays became wash days. I hung them down in the cellar on the clotheslines . . . his and my shorts, socks, handkerchiefs, bedclothes. He said he'd take his white shirts to the Chinese Laundry. On Tuesday evenings I'd iron what I'd washed the day before. Sunday morning . . . neither of us ever went to church . . . we shared dusting and vacuuming the house.

"Just in case she ever comes back," he said. "Neither of us can be ashamed."

Actually she would have been proud. And that was another incongruity, for after all that time, coming out of school one Monday as I was crossing the street, there she stood on the other side waiting for me.

"Mother," I cried. "What are you doing here?" She was all dressed up like she was a lady working in a downtown office, maybe even a bank teller, or the lady who took the electric-bill payments at West Penn Power offices.

"I wanted to see how you were getting along, Westley."

"Oh, I'm fine, Mother. And you?"

"I'm OK," she said. And she put her hand through my hair.

"You eating all right?"

"Oh, yeah, Pap and me . . . we're doing all right. When are you coming home?"

"You ask him that question," she smiled.

"Will it be soon, Mom?"

"Don't know," she says.

"Where you staying?"

"With your Aunt Christina," she said.

For the first time . . . I looked at her differently. In my mind I saw only that mummified woman swaddled in the plaid blanket wrapped like the Torah or some rolled-up manuscript lying stiffly next to my naked, arms-and-legs-akimbo, fun-loving father. But she didn't look that way now. There was rouge on her cheeks and she'd had her hair marcelled. She wore a pair of fancy shoes with tiny mother-of-pearl buttons, and the heels were especially high. Not the "sensible" kind she was used to wearing.

"Well, I must be going," she said. "I miss you, Westley."

"I miss you, too," I said.

"Did you ask him about that saying I asked you to?"

"Yes," I said.

"What'd he tell you?"

"It means '*Two people live together until one of them kills the other*,'" he said.

She laughed haughtily. Again unlike her. In the past it was usually a sniff at one of his wisecracks. Like she resented doing it. And while she was laughing she pulled me to her. Now I knew what Aunt Christina smelled like.

"You tell Daddy I seen you today," she said.

I watched her disappear up the side street and step into the rear seat of a fancy burgundy sedan.

That evening over dinner I told Pap. He appeared particularly interested. I wasn't sure he would be. We seemed to be getting along just fine. I liked it because there were no more rancorous fights between them. The house was very peaceful. He and I had become friends. Buddies kind of, like we enjoyed each other's quiet company. And we both got excited about looking forward to movies on Sunday night. We'd talk about these over dinner often.

But this night he grilled me about Mother. What'd she look like? What was she wearing? Did she look happy? Did she laugh? What did she say about me? Did she ask if I'd been drinking, going out every night? Every question he could think of. And when I told him she queried me about the *'Til Death Do Us Part* saying, and that'd I given his retort . . . he seemed to settle back in his chair as if he'd just won some big prize at the carnival. Or hooked a giant trophy fish . . . even though he never went.

Long after dinner nearly a week later, maybe nine o'clock, the dishes all cleaned up and Pap is still sitting at the kitchen table reading the newspaper. I am on the kitchen floor trying to repair an old toaster I'd salvaged from the cellar. I had my tool chest out and had the toaster all apart and was seeing how the coil was working. It was glowing a bright orange in my hands when I heard a knock at the kitchen door.

Father and I both looked up. I could see her face in the window.

"It's Mother!" I cried. He lifted the paper back up to his face. I opened the door.

"May I come in?" she said.

She was carrying this chrysanthemum-stenciled valise, and I took it from her as she stepped into the kitchen, closing the door behind her. I stood back, watching the two of them. He didn't lower the newspaper. She stood there wearing a strange grin and Aunt Christina's ankle-length fur coat, a black fox. Her lips were painted magenta as were her cheeks and her hair had a reflective dressing that caught the overhead light. It was Christina's perfume that quickly invaded the room. Some kind of incongruous magnetism was occurring between these two people that I didn't fully comprehend. I understood a lot by now about men and women—but I still hadn't understood everything.

"How have you been, Westley?" she said in a seductive manner. When I knew she was really speaking to Pap.

"Have you come back home, Ma?" I said.

"Well, it all depends," she replied.

"Depends on what?" I said.

"You ask him," she said.

I turned to Father. "Pap?"

He slowly lowered the paper, never looking at me, but studying her, from her high heels right up her stocking-free legs through the opening in the borrowed coat, then onto her hopeful face.

"Mother wants to know if she's welcome to stay." Attempting to broker this fractured affair.

"It depends."

"Depends on what, Joe?" She smiled.

"Depends on how fast you're willing to climb those stairs," he replied.

Without answering, Mother took off her wrap, leaned over to give me an aromatic kiss, and climbed the stairs to their bedroom. Moments passed after both of us heard the door being softly drawn shut. Father stood, said goodnight, asked me to be certain to turn off all the lights, and followed her up.

I fiddled with the toaster on the floor, going through the motions actually, awaiting the latch to engage the strike plate.

Then the real incongruity struck me, just as his barbs once did her. Hadn't she said I was the *real man of the house* over and over again? Hadn't I professed to her indeed all those years I was growing up *'Til Death Do Us Part, Mother*? Yet, Aunt Christina's fox lay draped over the dinette chair and the scent of jasmine lingered in our kitchen, more intoxicating than the onions and sardines.

Or even the red-veined eggs.

# BIG WHITEY

CYRUS QUINN WAS running out of money, fast. By the end of the week he'd be hungry. The *New York Post* classifieds were giving him no satisfaction. The cattle call for college-educated clerks by the telephone company was one half hour away. American Can, after indicating they wouldn't hire him, told him, "Don't wear a gingham shirt the next time."

He thought it was the philosophy major that queered it.

*Too intense. Stop thinking you're Marlon Brando. It makes personnel uncomfortable. Effect a sunny disposition. New York City is primally dark. Brighten the interviewer's office. Imagine you're a sunflower. Back Home in Indiana—have a tune in your heart.*

Uniformed Bell Telephone women clerks herded the applicants into a room the size of the New York City Public Library's reading room. Long collapsible tables with chairs on either side had been set up in tight rows. Three hundred applicants scribbled on forms while others awaited seats.

"How many openings?" Quinn asked one of the attendants.

"Thirty."

"When will we know?"

"We'll phone you within a week—if we're interested."

*I could have worn my gingham shirt. And what's this?*

Quinn sat down at the table—ten men on either side—and was handed a packet of papers. The first couple of pages asked for the standard information: education and work history. But then came the essay question.

> You are in a boat with two best friends. You can swim, they cannot. A storm arises and capsizes your craft. There are two life jackets. Do you:
>> A: Permit your two friends to have the life preservers?
>> B: Fight for one of the life preservers?
>> C: With a belt, lash the two wearing preservers and yourself together?

The question perplexed Quinn. A self-starter would pick *B*. However, Bell was jealous of its civic-minded image, so the answer had to be *A*. *I give the life preservers to my two very frightened friends and begin swimming.* Yet, it could be the collective approach, *C*, that required neither crass indifference nor chamber-of-commerce altruism. It underscored the need to work together.

Quinn looked about him. Each applicant had his head down and was either concentrating or dutifully acting, except a bespectacled, round-faced applicant (his collar had a yellowish cast to it, as did his teeth) glancing at him from across the table. Quinn couldn't understand the nature of the man's mincing smile. Returning to his task, he heard a whispered threat couched in base profanity and shot his head up only to encounter the character grinning ingratiatingly at him.

Quinn now became nervous. Each time he returned to the essay, the character ratcheted up his invectives. They assumed a sadistic tone. Cutting Quinn with a razor blade in the bathtub while the tormentor performed fellatio. He'd copulate Quinn with a Colt .45 while micturating into his mouth. Each time Quinn raised his head, the screed ceased, and the man exchanged that unnerving affectation of his, as if to say, "It ain't me you're hearing say that nasty stuff, buddy. Funny, though?"

Upset because he'd cut down his food intake to one meager meal a day, and now having to contend with a sweating pervert sitting across from him, Quinn summoned the attendant.

"Could there be two answers to this essay question, ma'am?"

"Pick one and give your reasons why."

"Of course there is only one answer," The tormentor volunteered. "Any ignoramus can see that," and, catching Quinn's eye, swiped his victim's pant leg with a pointed shoe. Quinn slid his chair out from the table and placed the exam on his lap.

*"Wait until this is over, cocksucker,"* the redolent character hissed. *"I'll follow you home and stick it down your throat while pinching Voltaire's nose, you yellow bastard!"*

The multiple choice essay would be a simple one if only you were one of the sailors, thought Quinn.

Distraught and wanting to vacate the building before the sadist, Quinn picked the community-spirited choice, and wrote a fulsome paragraph to the effect that, "Humankind must rise or fall together." The vitriol of his table partner had now become even more imaginative and terminally graphic. When Quinn looked up to confront his tormentor, the smile of denial had assumed a victor's glibness. Pretending to pen an additional passage, Quinn waited for the screed to resume, whereupon he shot up from the table, pressed the completed application into the attendant's hand, and, bypassing the elevator, looped down six flights of steps. On the street he sought refuge in a coffee shop, monitoring the plate glass window while huddled in a back booth. Minutes later, the sadist reappeared . . . his face obscenely mashed against the window, squinting for Quinn. Unable to see his proposed victim, he suddenly appeared grievously hurt and wandered off.

*The advantage of living in a big city like New York. The guy could ruin my life in a small town. What are the chances of my ever seeing him again? But food is running out. Money or one week's rooming-house rent. Car fare for one week. Then the first pint of blood to sell. Maybe if I try to get employment in an eatery. Ah, what's this?* "WHITE CASTLE HIRING, ALL SHIFTS. WE TRAIN."

Quinn immediately phoned.

"Do you have a prison record?" the receptionist asked.

"No."

"Are you free to work any hours any shift?"

"Yes. Days, nights . . . whenever."

The following day, Tuesday, (still no call from Bell) he stepped out of the elevator at the twenty-seventh floor of a Frank Sullivan flat-iron building in the thirties. Dozens of small offices on either side of the narrow hallway were occupied by lone accountants, lawyers, insurance salesmen, detectives, literary agents—all behind shellacked oaken portals with a riveleted translucent glass pane advertising the establishment's name in inelegant black letters. Room 143 read "E. A. Tully, Esq."

*Was this somebody's idea of a joke?*

A middle-aged woman wearing a cameo broach at her alabaster neck greeted Quinn. She gestured he take a seat. The chairs were tubular aluminum with green plastic seats like in a post office. A gun-metal gray desk, empty steel shelves, an Underwood typewriter propped before the secretary on a green felt blotter. Her dress looked like an Egon Schiele print.

"I presume you're Mr. Quinn."

The edges of his stiff white shirt were yellow, their armpits soiled.

"I did inquire if you have a prison record, didn't I Mr. Quinn?"

"Yes."

"And you said?"

"I have not."

"Mr. Tully will see you now, sir. Go through that door, please."

The door leading to Mr. Tully looked exactly like those in the hallway, an opaque plate glass window covering a third of its mass, but this one had neither letters nor numbers. Quinn bowed graciously to the receptionist and entered White Castle.

A tall, black gentleman with an anthracite beard and penetrating blue eyes stood fully attired in a chef's costume and a toque inscribed Big Whitey. Chromium counter stools with red leather seats abutted a Formica counter on which sat a glass case of freshly baked peach, raisin, lemon meringue and apple pies. Salt-white hexagonal tiles inlaid with White Castle in glass-black script covered the floor. Mr. Tully assumed his post behind the counter in front of the large grill, blue and yellow gas jets illuminating its undersides. An orange drink bubbler sat at the far end of the counter gurgling. Posters of Big Whitey hamburgers being devoured by cartoon men and women adorned the pale-green windowless walls, and the coin-operated, chromium juke box selector attached to the counter sat blank except for Charlie Parker's *Repetition*.

"Mr. Quinn, slip into this uniform, please."

Tully handed Quinn a striped pair of cotton pants, a freshly laundered white shirt, a black leather bow tie, an apron and a toque. He pointed to the restroom. Even that was a mock-up of what existed in every White Castle he'd ever patronized. An "Employees Wash Hands Before Leaving," sign hung above the toilet.

"Call me Professor," Tully joked, as he made the first hamburger, then had Quinn slavishly copy him.

"All Whiteys, big or small, are prepared with finely chopped onions whether the customer wants them or not. It's why they taste so damn good." Tully rolled the ground meat in his thick hands as if it were fresh snow, then he'd slap it flat. Each time another burger was fried, it was tossed into the trash. Soon, he began cracking eggs with the one-hand method. First, a smart thrust to a hard surface, then with index finger and thumb, while the hand swooped to the skillet, the yolk and albumen were released unmarried. Again and again, Quinn cracked the eggs against the skillet, arm lifted aloft as if he were a pianist then authoritatively down, dropping the unbroken yokes into the melting slab of butter—*Banjo Eyes*.

"By spooning the hot butter over the yokes until they whiten, barely, you make *Eddy's Asleep*. Tully taught as if he were a maestro of dance.

"It's all in the wrists. Showmanship. Your customers watching your every move." Tully was a stickler for neatness, too. "This is no science, Quinn. It's kid's stuff. You're Big Whitey, remember. Now onto *Mulligan's Jewels*."

Quinn had no idea how long he and the "Professor" had been at the grill with the absence of daylight to indicate the passage of time. He presumed it must have been four or five hours. Finally, the mentor removed his apron and toque and took a seat at the counter, opened a menu, looked up at Quinn and ordered lunch.

"Two *Big Whiteys* with *Ivories*, a side of *Mulligan's Jewels, Frank Capra's* for my wife (he didn't have one), and one *Manage a Trois*. Oh, and a slice of *Uncle Whisker's*. Light on the *Moo* in our *Wake-ups*, please."

The student nonplussed stared at Tully. But went immediately to work, attempting to recall Tully's invented jargon for the various plates on the menu. ("Remember you're in the entertainment business.") And despite his forgetting a step or two, got it all right except the splats. They were a little battery in their centers. Tully sloughed it off.

"The wife won't eat them all anyway. I don't know why the hell she insists on ordering them." He laughed and swept all the prepared food into the rubbish bin.

Quinn cleaned up after himself.

"Now you sit, Mr. Cyrus, and tell me. You must be hungry."

*Jesus, is this God behind the counter? I get to eat already?* He ordered exactly the same as the professor, except he passed on the flapjacks and omelet but wanted ice cream on his apple pie.

"I'll get those dance steps down cold, Mr. Tully, don't worry."

"Oh, I'm sure you will. There's one more very important thing I want to tell you, son."

"What's that, sir?"

"You're no longer Cyrus Quinn."

Quinn looked at him puzzled.

"Whitey . . . always Big Whitey. We come in two sizes—Whiteys and Big Whiteys. (the Whiteys were a quarter and the Big Whiteys 35 cents, 40 cents with cheese or "ivories") When the customer says, "I want a Whitey," you respond, "Big Whitey, sir?" And when they say they want a hamburger, you say, 'One Big Whitey on the Fry!'

"You get it?"

"Yessir," said Quinn. He liked this kindly professor. This was a bonafide hamburger school. And when he finished eating, Tully disappeared for several minutes, returning with a diploma that had a black satin ribbon attached.

> Cyrus Quinn, this 17th day of November, 1961, successfully graduated from White Castle Hamburger Institute.
> signed, E. A. Tully, Director.

"What's your first name, Mr. Tully, if you don't mind my asking?"

"Tony's my middle. Eaustis is my first. It's my little joke, Quinn. Up here on the 27th floor for the last eleven years cooking hamburgers, spuds and eggs and tossing them into the can. Boring as hell. Two shifts each day, one morning and one afternoon. What did you major in college, Quinn?"

"Philosophy."

"None of my business, son. No prison time?"

"No sir."

"New York University, 1938. *Summa Cum Laude*. Masters in hydraulic engineering. Strange where the tide of life tosses you sometimes, huh, son? 'Course I don't want to inquire into the reasons how you ended up here. But you won't go hungry. And you sure can be anonymous. Big Whitey, remember? Nobody expecting a philosophy major to be beating his eggs. Do you smoke, Mr. Quinn?"

"Yessir."

"Well, join me." The two men sat in the lone booth. Tully got up and fed coins into the music box.

"When do I go to work, sir?"

"This evening, 125th Street, eleven-to-seven shift. They'll be having you bubble dancing 'n working the counter for a day or two, then you'll be on the flames."

"Am I a short order cook?"

"Yeah, that's what you are, son. You religious, Quinn?"

"What do you mean?"

"Do you profess a belief in God?"

"Like now maybe?"

"All those philosophy courses didn't queer you on the notion, huh?"

Quinn laughed.

"I'm a Rosicrucian myself. If you're a critical thinker—like I suspect you are, Mr. Quinn—you might want to give it some consideration."

Mr. Tully quietly finished his cigarette, stood, and shook Quinn's hand. "I get damn lonesome back in here. It would be a lot more interesting if I had people walking in off the street. You had no idea, did you, Quinn, what was behind that door?"

"I expected a man in a dark suit behind another gray desk, sir. I never expected to enter a nobody and exit Big Whitey."

Both men laughed.

"Anonymity, son. I'm *Big Whitey*, you're *Big Whitey*. Powdered flapjacks are *Frank Capras, Uncle Whiskers*—apple pie. Nothing's ever as it appears to be, son. You see the humor in it after you be showing up here every morning for work as I have for the past decade, saying hello to spinster Grace—she's been here at White Castle school for twenty-seven years!—and opening a restaurant that's never had one damn paying customer."

Quinn hesitated then asked. "Why do you do it, Mr. Tully?"

"I could ask the same of you, boy." He laughed heartily. Cyrus could see his massive chest and biceps straining the White Castle issued shirt.

"You made my day, Professor, in fact my month." He walked into the outer room, then turned to glance back at Mr. Tully who was sitting on the counter stool inserting another coin for the Bird-with-strings tune.

"One more question, sir."

"What is it, Quinn?"

"Would you've hired me if I had a record?"

"What'd you do, boy?"

"Nothing. But suppose I had?"

"Big Whiteys got no past. When I slid your Frank Capras into the trash barrel, so went Cyrus Quinn. You're Big Whitey now. To me 'n anybody else from here on out on the opposite side of the counter. *You've just been saved, son.*"

\* \* \*

His first night's work, Quinn washed dishes when he wasn't wait-ing the counter. The eleven p.m. to two a.m. spell saw nonstop traf-fic. Three to five a.m.—maybe a dozen customers in all. None of the staff spoke to Quinn other than to issue orders. At five-thirty the establishment was overflowing.

"Two Wake-ups to go, light on the Moo!"

"One Big Honkey with!"

"Humpty Dumptys with toast."

"Fruit Cakes!"

Tully's colorful substitutes stayed in the 27th floor two-room suite. Each site had it's own lingo. One hour before his quitting time Quinn was told by the manager to take all the wooden slat sections on which the counter people walked, outside into the street to hose and scrub down for the next shift. During the slow two-to-five period he mopped the white tile floor. At no time this first evening did anyone call him Big Whitey.

One week passed at various sites: two nights at 125th Street, one at 57th Street on the west side, three in Jackson Heights. (There they called him "Bernie.") Each shift Quinn mostly cleaned and did janitorial work, only occasionally getting behind the counter. But he was no longer hungry and the anxiety about having to pay his rent eased.

His second week of work began at the end of the Van Court-land Park subway line. A White Castle stood alongside two Irish bars at the base of the hill that lead to Manhattan College and several Riverdale private secondary schools. Here the traffic flow was more modest, heating up a little before midnight and keeping steady until one-thirty. It became very quiet until six and then re-mained steady but manageable throughout the remainder of the morning. Quinn was summoned to work the grill.

He'd fallen into a pleasant rhythm after several shifts at the same location. Regulars were beginning to refer to him as Whit-ey. It didn't happen automatically. The customers only used the appellation if they felt a sense of familiarity. Occasionally an ine-briated customer would call out Big Whitey as a taunt. And his expertise at the grill was becoming more refined, his technique polished. (*"Remember, son, first you're an entertainer."*) It was especially important that his costume for the evening be freshly starched, and he took caution to keep it from becoming soiled throughout the shift.

There was an extreme sense of gratification Quinn was taking from doing a job exceptionally well. A short order cook, albeit with a limited repertoire. During the slow period he and the counterman might converse, but mostly he fed the Wurlitzer, having bribed the vendor to place the same recordings he had at the 125th Street location in his 244th Street stop.

"The Micks will have your balls, Whitey. You shitting me?"

"Maybe we'll educate the bastards," Quinn insisted.

Billy Holiday, Dexter Gordon, The Prez, Bird, Jimmy Lunceford's band, Monk, Duke, Ella, Dizzy, Bud Powell . . . it's how Quinn spent his tips.

* * *

Until the second month, sometime after two a.m. Quinn stood leaning up against the counter, his back turned to the stools, staring out at the traffic on Broadway and listening to his tunes, when a stranger entered, sat down at the far end of the counter, and slid a menu out of its chromium grip. Quinn's counterman had retired to the restroom with the *Daily News*.

"What will it be, sir?"

"I'm thinking. Give me a coffee."

"Cream and sugar?"

"Neither."

"Yessir. One Wake-up coming right up." *Jesus, the guy looks familiar. Where in the hell have I seen him before?* "Anything else?"

The customer didn't lift his head. "One poached egg on toast," he said.

"Sally Takes a Bath on the Square!" Quinn cried, and filled a poaching pan with water, which he quickly brought to a boil, then carefully lowered the egg into one of four rounds. Shortly he stood before the customer with the poached egg of perfect consistency, soon to bleed sun-like on the buttered toast. The stranger looked up and smiled gratuitously at him.

*"We miss you at The Bell,"* he simpered.

Quinn turned pale.

The customer lowered his head to eat. "The persimmon trees in the park are lovely in wintertime, Mr. Quinn. I'll draw our bath and await you under the El."

The restroom door opened, and the counterman, with the *News* sticking out of his back pocket, resumed his station. Bird blew the last bar of *Ornithology*. Quinn, stricken, leaned against the grill and stared out into the night.

"Can I get you anything else?" the counterman asked.

"Not this time," the stranger answered. And rose to leave, humming to the chef:

*"Bloody Whitey on our Sails, Spinoza. I'll hold the moo."*

# SAY HELLO TO STANLEY

BUDDY HART HAULED the Hammond B-3 in a two-wheel trailer hitched to his father's Willys sedan. The family thought Uncle Stanley's talent as a barrel-house pianist had by some mysterious route passed down to Bud. And the miracle became even more fortuitous when Stanley lost two of his fingers in the cutting mill along with his gig.

The skaters loved Buddy's jazz-riff music. He'd imitate their gliding, pumping motion as they rounded the back wall of the Hi-Way Roller Dome smiling up at him in the open air booth that cantilevered the skate floor. The more venturesome rollers who executed the "Backslider," "Alice Goes to Market," or the "Janey Mae," he'd tease with several bars of *Salt Peanuts*. And Buddy sounded just like Chet Baker singing when he'd accompany himself on a ballad.

But on Saturday and Sunday night at the Bluebird Inn, no microphone banter accompanied his riffs. This playing was dead real. He dug into the organ's bed for inspiration, and when he got real hot, he'd grab a *D minor b5* chord in the upper register and sit on the damn thing for two unrelenting, screaming B-3 minutes. Buddy opened up Ohio's skies with a machete, for Chrissake.

"Ain't he one mean dude!" a lady cried. "Sing, Buddy. Sing. Oh my God!"

The sweat rolling off Buddy's boy face, Chet Baker tears, dripping summery onto the Hammond B-3's keyboard.

What a white black musician he was. Uncle Stanley reserved a table every Saturday night to watch his nephew. Then Celia Hubbard, a twenty-three year old auburn-haired socialite, began showing up. Her presence added a certain *je ne sais quoi* to the bar, and at evening's close, she'd fold a fresh twenty dollar bill in a glass Buddy kept on the organ. Celia drove a 1948 Nash Convertible, one of 750 ever manufactured in America.

"She walks in here like it were a salon," Peewee, the Bluebird's owner, said. "Do you watch all the women eyein' her, Buddy? I ain't ever seen a red snatch, have you?"

"She just digs the organ, man."

"I didn't mean no disrespect," Peewee nodded. "But she lights this place up like your music, Buddy. What you say her name was?"

"Celia Hubbard."

"Where she from?"

"East Jesus."

"Don't shit me, man."

"Patterson."

"Uh Huh." It made sense. Patterson, outside Warren, was an enclave for the rich. Homes on lots of several acres, many of them with their own barns and grazing horses.

"Her father invented the drinking fountain, Peewee."

"Jesus, yes? You see that damn car she's driving?"

"I been in it, Peewee. Cream leather seats, still smells new inside too."

"Where you go, Buddy?"

"Over to the Glass Hat to catch Jolly's last set." Jolly Patchen was the local blues singer and guitarist many believed was better than John Lee Hooker, but who never made it out of Warren.

"She taking an eye to you, Buddy?" Peewee asked.

"Shit, I'm just a skate-wheel musician, man," he replied.

* * *

The day Buddy ceased playing for the Rollerdrome all the regulars sat on the skate floor, the mirror ball chasing magenta, heliotrope, indigo and mustard-yellow lights circling the grand hanger in darkness, mechanical fireflies all on permanent tethers . . . It was the strangest melancholic night, almost masochistic for Buddy and the crowd. Some of the rollers had been attending regularly for the six years Buddy'd been playing. It wasn't the skating so much as his cherubic face, his boyish laughter and his Chet Baker's girl-voice ballads that kept them coming back.

He was moving onto the big time now. No more sweat effluvium wafting up the skate floor, the silly mechanical *pas de deux*, the skate-dancing charades, the maestros who only chose to dance alone. Forty-year-old women with hair freshly dyed and sculpted up like an Eiffel tower, their sequined skate costumes causing the colored lights to swirl on their derrières like the mirror ball on the ceiling. Or the men with pompadour-hair and cigarette packs—Lucky Strikes mostly—rolled up in their tee shirt sleeves, tight trousers held up by plastic belts, doing those leaps into the air to the beat of Buddy's sweet music, lost in their odeons, barbers and telephone clerks by days, stars in the Rollerdrome orbit at night—Oh, God, he wouldn't miss them . . .

They wanted Buddy to sing to them. He had this "wish board" up in his booth that controlled every light on the floor, the speed of the mirror ball, the speaker system. Buddy Hart, the Master of the *mise en scène*, the Harlin County Artaud, the Rollerdome wizard. Tonight they wanted Chet Baker.

The giant mirror-faced moon he ratcheted down to a drug-induced revolution, the thousand shards of light-illuminated flies with mirror backs, all the colors of a dreamer's rainbow, and the B-3 began to drone, in the lower register, a reedy vibrato. Buddy wasn't Jimmy Smith no more. Instead a lachrymose idol. Up there in the booth hovering over them. Long mournful *ommmmmms*.

As if he wanted to purge them with a colonic of sadness. The audience watched the flies circle the wall and the floors. Like some kind of star calliope jar they were inside, except lying on the floor looking up at the hangar steel-trussed heavens. Christ, it was strange out there on route I-27 on the outskirts of Niles, a dink copper-refinery town, its sulfurous odor hanging over the valley like a scrim. The skaters with their red-and-white yarn pom-poms on the toes of their skate-shoes parked forlornly alongside them.

And just when it became almost unbearable, Buddy began to sing "When Sonny Gets Blue" in his best Chet Baker voice . . . followed by "Nature Boy" and then—the surprise of the evening— "The Little White Cloud That Cried." He was warbling like he was a damn skater, too; that he wasn't any different than those folks down on the floor, surrendering to melancholy and nostalgia, ignorant of complicated chord changes, technique, and awesome Bud Powell lines . . . the stuff of the cognoscenti. Surely if Peewee were in this audience of colorfully laced skaters with pom-poms on their shoes and Waveset in their hair, he'd stab the keyboardist out of his self-indulgent stupor.

"'Little Things Mean A Lot,' Buddy!" one sequined matron bellowed up from under his booth. Buddy smiled his oleaginous grin and began tapping the tune into the Hammond B-3. Several of the women yanked the pompons off their skates, tossing them up into Buddy's open box. The yarn balls rained on the organ bouncing down to its pedals.

Christ, what if Celia came in, thought Buddy. A shiver went up his spine. "Lady's Choice!" he hollered, and beat out the "Beer Barrel Polka." The mirror ball spun rapidly, its mechanical flies with mirror backs circling the skater's hall like traffic on a freeway. It took sometime for the crowd to catch up. But they did. The crowd now circled the hanger like plastic fish in an arcade's Fish-Until-You-Catch-A-Winner trough. The calliope!

But the Harts lived on DeForest road where the toilets, bathtubs, sinks, washing machines, all flushed into an open sewer. Barely a half dozen houses away alongside the railroad tracks sat one of the most notorious cathouses this side of Cleveland. (His mother worked as a nurses aid on weekends, turning patients over in their beds like flapjacks.) What the hell was he doing messing around with this woman whose father invented the drinking fountain?

"I'll take away all your financial worries," Celia urged. "You can devote as much time as you wish to your music . . . what do you say?"

"Jesus, we hardly know each other."

"What's there to know?" she said. Then embarrassed him by asking, "Sex?"

He didn't respond.

"Say it, Mr. Hart. If it's sex you're wondering about, I got all that you want, too. Anything for you, Buddy."

Every poor man's dream come alive, a red-haired one no less with a magenta labial shrub. That and dollars, too, thousands of them. A sleek automobile instead of the old man's turtle of a Willy's. Horses. What the hell was the catch?

When Buddy mentioned it to his father, Rupert said, "Fuck her if you want, but don't marry her, Son. You'll be worse off than your Uncle Stanley. When she's finished working you over, you'll sound like Johnny Ray. You like auburn cooz?"

"How do you know she got red hair, Pap?"

"Every man in Harlan County's got a wet dream off Celia Hubbard at one time or another. 'Cept you're the unfortunate one." Buddy's mother just shook her head. She walked over to the kitchen sink, opened the faucet, and began scrubbing her fingernails with a vegetable brush.

\* \* \*

When the newlyweds returned from the Bahamas, an indigo-blue Chrysler station wagon convertible sat parked in Celia's driveway. Eustace Hubbard even suggested Buddy begin working in the corporate offices, and sent him off to his haberdasher for a fitting. Just like the movies. Buddy's kid sisters couldn't quite believe his good fortune. And within a year of the wedding the Hi-Way Rollerdrome closed for lack of business. Peewee began politicking Buddy to gig at the Bluebird every night. But that venue become more irregular. The Hammond B-3 sat at the ready covered over with a bed sheet on the back of the bandstand. Following one of the performances, Peewee asked why Stanley never showed anymore.

"No idea," Buddy said.

"Your old friends. They gone, too."

"It's botherin' you, Peewee?"

"She's watered you down, Buddy."

Buddy glowered.

"You dig, pal? Excuse the disrespect, but the cunt's dimmed your lights."

"Cut the shit, Peewee."

"Can't, brother. I known you too long. First a red-haired snatch. Then a yellow one. A magenta one. Puce. Goddamnit, the gash are gonna dry you up like the foreskin on a cadaver. Tonight, yeah, I could hear echoes of old Buddy Hart in there. But you just coastin' man. That rich shit is dragging you down. You ain't got the drive no more."

"You saying you don't want me playing the Bluebird no more, Peewee?"

"Buddy Hart's always welcome here."

"She's my wife." Buddy stood and headed for the doorway.

"Yeah, and her old man's that drinking fountain hanging on our shithouse wall, too! Come back to the tunes, man. *And say hello to STANLEY!*"

\* \* \*

It's true, thought Buddy, traveling back to Patterson alone that night—no trailer on the hitch—having to pass the boarded-up Rollerdrome with its mirror-ball heaven that once moved and bounced to his B-3. He hadn't seen Stanley. Or many of his other friends. But now he wasn't a shiny-ass piano man playing for a couple of dollars in bars reeking of disinfectant either.

So what if I'm Celia Hubbard's boy. Huh? Don't have to worry about nothing no more. Chet Baker, Johnny Ray, Jimmy Smith, Bud Powell . . . Christ, none of that shit bothers me. I fucking got it made. Fuck Stanley. Let him chop his index finger and thumb off, the ungrateful bastard. Celia and I offered to help. But the bastard's too poor . . . fucking jealous. One of us got lucky.

Just then the Chrysler came to a dead stop. He and Peewee had been drinking—that was new, too. But what the hell. He drank his shit. Screw the powder. He looked down at the dashboard and ground the starter several times, pumping on the accelerator. The engine wouldn't catch. The bitch's dry, he thought. Then Buddy saw a hot moon barreling straight for him. He fumbled with the window handle. It kept swinging on him, not catching like it should have.

"What the fuck's gone wrong!" he cried. "Open up you cocksucker. Open up!" The engine caught the Chrysler's front end, dragging the car several hundred yards up the track, screeching to a halt. A screaming screech. *Ab* of the B-3, Buddy thought, lying on the floorboards. This is fucking scary. That never was.

Soon the engineer and several track men were pounding on the windshield: "Are you alright, mister? Speak to us. Can you hear us?" Once outside, Buddy watched the water spit through his radiator's chromium teeth, the automobile's remaining headlight still shone and the horn stuck.

"Christ, I'm fine," he sighed. "Ain't a goddamn thing wrong with me, boys. Thanks for stopping," he said, and let out a Chet Baker laugh.

\* \* \*

The ride downhill went damn fast after that. "I don't like wearing suits all day," he told Eustace Hubbard one spring morning, who replied, "You either be one of us, boy, or none of us."

"I'll take the latter," Buddy says, and parked his and Celia's new car in Hubbard's driveway, then hiked back to their house in Patterson.

Now and then he'd get a call for a gig. But he'd show up for a set in the bag, forget the damn chord changes, and the rare club that did hire him kept back-up musicians—brass on the stage—who could take over when he slid.

Nobody saw Celia much anymore either. She looked weird, her hair unkempt and lips darker than they ever were. Almost black now. She'd rouge her sallow cheeks with a magenta color. Folks thought she resembled some kind of mythical bird—her shoulders stooped over like a carrion eater's—who glided in and out of town when she walked. Word had it that she began to drink as much as Buddy did. That the two of them would start in the morning and work through several bottles by day's end. At dusk they'd mount the horses stark naked.

The grocery delivery boy would buzz to be let in. Soiled dishes lay piled everywhere. He stopped putting milk or butter in the refrigerator, for food in there had rotted, causing an unbearable stench.

"Can you hear any music being played in the house, Cal?" Charley Tompkins, the owner of Patterson Market, asked the boy.

"Sounded like some adolescent kid, like me maybe, Charley, you know unable to make the higher keys, a kind of voice like that coming from the bedroom and a sad trumpet sound." Sure, thought Charley Tompkins.

* * *

Several months later that July, Rupert woke Myra over on DeForest Road one midnight. "Someone's down pounding our door."

"You're hearing things."

"Damnit, I ain't!" he barked, slipping on his pants. He shambled down the stairs and saw a form on the other side of the curtained oval. "Who is it?" he asked. "Whadaya want?"

"It's Celia," came the reply.

Rupert was stunned. "Just a minute," he says, fumbling with the key in the lock. Celia stood before him looking frightened, weary and bundled in one of Buddy's camel hair overcoats. This flower has faded fast, he thought. Like one of those pretty things in his perennial garden that overnight becomes a shadow of its promise the day earlier, and three days later goes to seed. Fucking drinking fountain daughters. Same as copper smelt mill daughters and sons, fucking babies of the rich, all fair and shallot stocks for spines.

"Jesus, what is it, Celia? You look bad."

"Is Myra here?" she asked.

"Yes. What is it?"

"Tell her to come quick."

Rupert seeing the woman's urgency, he'd been ordered about like this before—yells up to Myra. "Mommy, get down here quick!"

Myra comes running down the stairway with a nightgown covering her naked body like a sheer curtain, then, seeing Celia, draws it to her. "What is it, Honey? You sick?"

"I am, Myra. I'm sick as a dog."

"Where's Bud?"

"Don't know. Does anybody, for Chrissake?"

Rupert understood. Buddy was probably out in some other woman's bed. What else? The money eatin' away at him like green cancer. Alexander Hamilton cancer.

Myra was solicitous. The young woman was in pain. No time to be thinking about any hurt or anger now.

Celia stared intensely at Myra, trying to answer her.

"Oh, shit. No, child!"

Celia nodded *yes*.

"Rupert, go put the kettle on for hot water quick! And get me some towels. They're down on the line. Grab every damn one of them. And hurry, Rupe, hurry!" Myra put her arm around Celia and rushed her up the stairs.

Rupert knew what this was about, too. What else could it be? No surprises in this life. Were there ever any? So the kid falls into a cesspool of greenbacks and gorges himself, fucks himself up and everything he touches . . . including this once beautiful breeze of a woman. Yeah, breeze, that's all she was. Fragile. Swept around the corner and cooled him off, smelling of magnolia and leather, Kentucky blue grass, clean underwear and stockings every goddamn day, and food in the cupboards—the pitcher of milk, this auburn haired breeze now shivering before Myra upstairs, vomiting her guts out in the toilet, her skin yellow as the shit carpet in our hallway, naked, the fluid dripping off her white breasts and rivuleting through her labial auburn forest with death. For that's surely what this night was going to be.

I can goddamn tell. Oh shit. A water death. Fuck you, Buddy ...

Rupert screamed to nobody in the kitchen, and the tea kettle begin to scream, too, but unlike the engine that caught Buddy's lucky-ass Chrysler, or the *Ab* on the B-3—this one pierced like a bird of doom gone mad and flapping about on the kitchen ceiling trying to ascend, to escape this birth house of Buddy Hart on De-Forest Road. Screaming Celia upstairs now echoing the tea kettle's noise, she's a bird up there, too. Rupert could hear a body slapping about on the tile floor of their bathroom. Like a fish now pulled out of the water still alive. The screaming and her flapping her white legs and arms against the tile walls and linoleum bathroom floor. Screaming. Screaming the B-3. Only this got under Rupert's skin. And he turned cold.

"Goddamn it, hurry, Rupe! Hurry up here for chrissake!"

Rupert rushed up the stairs, teapot steaming in one hand, towels in the other, the bathroom door wide open and Celia now moaning, her legs wide open and Myra naked too down on her knees on the floor dragging something out of Celia.

Oh yeah, Christ, he'd been there. Do I have to watch this, Jesus? he thought. Fuck Buddy. Fuck Bud Powell. Fuck Jimmy Smith. "Oh Ray Charles," he cried. "Ray Fucking Charles."

Then there was this loud UMMPH.

Like Myra had smashed a thick round pole into Celia's abdomen. But it wasn't that. There were two things lying on the bathroom floor, beating like hearts. They were wiggling, and kind of looked like something human, but maybe like fish, Rupert couldn't tell. He was down on his knees, thinking he was going to faint. The teapot on the floor next to him. Steaming. Christ, he was going to pass out. Hold onto me, he kept saying to himself. Hold onto me. Jesus. What those on the floor? Who are they, Myra? Jesus Christ. What's she brought home? Fuck you, Buddy. Fuck you.

Myra bit the cords.

Then turned on her haunches to see Rupert dumbly staring at her on his knees. Christ, he looks like a circus bear in shock, she thought. And slammed the bathroom door shut.

"Let me see 'em," moaned Celia.

"Ain't nothing there except water and blood, honey," Myra said soothingly. "It's all over, dear. Put your head back down. Close your eyes. Let me wash off your face with a cool rag."

Then Rupert heard nothing more till the toilet flushed. Twice.

\* \* \*

"I saw Buddy a week ago," Stanley told Rupert. "He invited me over to hear his Dexter Gordon Paris recordings."

"He have anything to say?" Rupe and Myra hadn't heard from Celia or Buddy since that fateful evening.

"Everything's fine. Claims he's gigging weekends in Cleveland again. They're thinking about having babies. He's bloated up like the Hindenburg. And full of shit. I can't blame it all on Celia, Rupe."

"I agree," Rupert said.

"Damn depressing. She took me into their *boudoir* to show off her new 'Louis the Fifteenth' bedroom set. Seems like every six months she tosses the *old* furniture into the barn and goes shopping for new. This bed and dresser weren't ugly enough, Rupe. You know what she did?"

"What?"

"Painted it sapphire. The gallon of wall paint and brush scumming up in the hallway. Mother's-Day sapphire. You think it's going to smell like some old patootie's dusted bosom when you stand next to it. And 'round the mirror's frame—she painted that, too, sloping it over onto the glass like she smears lipstick onto her teeth."

"I said it was going to sour quick, didn't I?" Rupe said.

"We all kind of guessed it, but none of us wanted to believe it."

"Because all you bastards thought you were going to get rich, too! That old Eustace was going to come over here and drop a trailer-load of cash in your driveways. Well, he has. But it ain't cash, brother. Money's a plague, I tell you.

"Stanley, if there's just one goddamn quarter left in my trouser pockets on my death bed, I promise I'll swallow the fucker before I take my last breath. I ain't leaving anybody *shit*. They'll all be better off."

Stanley could only shake his head.

\* \* \*

Buddy Hart got up early a Saturday morning that September to begin packing his belongings in a trunk he'd hauled up from the basement, one of the old metal and wood variety fashioned for journeys to Europe on ocean liners. Celia kept hers down the cellar to store toys.

She was still asleep, hung over from a session with Buddy the night before. At some point before dawn, it all became clear to him. None of this was fun anymore. In fact it was ugly. He missed the Bluebird Inn, even the old Hi-Way Rollerdrome. And it was more than nostalgia. People were talking. Maybe he could turn his life around. A caricature of old Buddy Hart stared back at him in the mirror. Some men might choose to put a bullet through their heads, he mused. There were several rifles out in the barn. Eustace Hubbard had taken him clay pigeon shooting. Now he at least knew how to load the gun and blow his head off. Didn't take much of a shot.

Yeah. And so what if Buddy Hart never made the lights outside Ohio? Jolly never did either. "Ain't fucking enough lights to go around, Hart," Jolly joked.

A lot of wisdom in that, too, Buddy agreed. I just got to get out of the nest. I don't need this booze shit. I liked things well enough before.

One gig. I'll get one gig. Clean my act up 'n' move onto the next.

And just as he was piling his sheet music into the trunk, Celia appeared in the hallway, naked, looking like a raven wraith.

Buddy broke into an ironic grin. Looking down at her stomach. Thinking how he and other men had dreamed about the auburn grove. It wasn't so pretty now. The day before she'd painted his baby grand piano—a wedding gift from Eustace—tomato red. Buddy cried when he saw it.

"Where do you think you're going?"

"Heading out, Celia."

"Oh, no," she said.

"We'll see each other," he soothed. "Why don't you work on the house here while I'm gone. Paint the kitchen cabinets. The floor, I don't give a good goddamn. I need air, Celia. The Hubbards are stealing my oxygen."

"You . . . Bunny Berrigan?" she laughed. "You going to go back to DeForest-by-the-Open-Sewer? All the shit of man in the gully outside your house, Buddy? Nothing that ain't been flushed down there." She lifted a cigarette off the coffee table and collapsed into the sofa. Buddy emptied the top drawer of his bureau where he kept his cuff links, wristwatch, and money clips—all Hubbard gifts—into the trunk.

"You ain't leaving," she said.

Buddy turned to her. "I am, Celia. It's been goddamn interesting and in the beginning, fun."

Celia stood. She offered Buddy a cigarette and lifted a chromium Statue of Liberty lighter off the glass coffee table, lighting it for him. It was as if she suddenly changed moods. Commiserative, helpful, solicitous. It's how she was in the beginning. Nothing she wouldn't do for Buddy Hart.

"What you got in there, honey?" she said.

Christ, what's this about? he thought. She gonna let me go? Hot damn. And he bent over the trunk, grasping its edge at the metal rasp with his melody hand, and with the bass-driver, pointed towards the sheet music, when, without warning, Celia slammed the lid shut, causing to erupt from Buddy Hart, alias Chet Baker, alias Jimmy Smith, alias Johnny Ray, a big piercing Hammond B-3 vibrato—*Ab diminished seventh*. Along with the clothes, the spare change and the costume jewelry, now lay Buddy Hart's middle finger. The Hammond B-3 screaming one.

*"And say hello to Stanley,"* she crooned.

# *HORACE*

"*A*S WIDE AS you can make it without makin' him a simpleton, put a smile on Tony's face," Jennie instructed Jimmy DiCarlo, the undertaker. "I don't want no goddamn phoney tears to mar his tie."

"He was a happy man, always happy, Jennie," Jimmy offered gratuitously.

"Always," she replied. "I'll miss the old bastard."

That night Jennie gathered his golf clubs, a fresh deck of cards and a bottle of Johnny Walker, and placed them alongside Anthony Prioletti, who, ready to greet the mourners, was all decked out in a seersucker suit, a stiff white shirt, and red satin tie.

"For Jennie Prioletti's sake" is how my mother put it when she dragged me to the mortuary the following day. It was my first experience seeing a formerly live person in a casket, and the place was bustling with Tony's cronies laughing and drinking champagne. Jennie worked the room like the Mayor. Tony's face glowed salmon, the shade of the gladioli sprays nimbusing his head. He looked like he was napping on the back seat of a chartered bus, heading to a Sons of Italy golf tournament in the sky. Soon they'd break out the cards and the galvanized garbage containers of iced beer.

Death isn't so scary after all, I concluded. Why was I worried about coming down with bulbar polio and dying in an iron lung? The Paramount—our only theatre—stopped its feature reel in the middle those years; the ushers would sweep up the aisles soliciting donations for the "Stop Polio!" campaign. On the screen they'd parade National Guard armories crowded with young children like myself confined to round steel cylinders that looked like oversized hot water heaters.

Then Patrick McCart, my friend from a couple streets over, and I spent a Saturday morning with our beebee guns shooting alley-cat rats up at the city dump located half mile up Cascade Street. The dump was always smoldering like biblical pictures of Hell. In some spots the flames geysered into the sky, especially if a new load of combustible material was dumped over the gorges by one of the many refuse trucks that trundled up and down our street night and day. A century earlier it had been a limestone quarry. There were great chasms, land shelves with precipitous dropoffs. Over decades water filled these quarries but eventually was displaced by the city's debris. Now trucks would just back up to one of the ledges and unload. Periodically haulers would drop explosive material over the dump. Fireworks! Strange patterns shooting meteor-like through the sky. I lay in bed at night waiting for the eruptions up in the quarry hills. Always the acrid odor from the dump made us cough and spit.

I thought that's how air smelled until we visited my Aunt Evelyn on the west side of Hebron. Mother, Aunt Evelyn, and I would sit out under the willow tree in her back yard in the summer time doing needlework, embroidering pansies and petunias on the wide hems of pillowcases for wedding and shower gifts. Aunt Evelyn gave me a basket of colored threads with wooden hoops and taught me how to make a giant needle-work sunflower. I practiced on my Uncle's handkerchief.

Uncle Ed drove an ice cream truck. Occasionally when I'd pass him on the street, he'd stop, get out of his truck, walk to the back and open its freezer door—the truck was built like a refrigerator—and hand me a Klondike bar. I thought about that out there with the two women, we're all making flowers on white percale, nobody saying a word, the monarch butterflies landing about our feet . . . and no garbage smoke. I thought this was heaven, too.

Then I see Patrick McCart's ashen face staring accusingly at me from the rear of DiCarlo's ambulance one late afternoon following school. I ran home to inquire of my mother what'd happened. "Polio," she said. "His mother had just made him curtains for his bedroom, too—white sheets with red hulls and royal-blue sails. Patrick came home ill from school."

It was the damn mayonnaise. He and I'd been horsing around throwing cans, tossing disgusting debris at each other that morning three months back at the city dump. I found a rotting jar of mayonnaise, scooped it out with a stick, then lobbed it at him. The glop smacked him on his cheek, causing him to retch. Our laughter stopped. Patrick wanted to go home. He never made it into the water heater.

* * *

Aunt Evelyn had this neighbor friend, his name was Horace, about forty years old, same as my aunt, the son of Mrs. McCool in the neighboring house. One day when I went visiting her on my own, she said we should call Horace to come down and see us. We cut through the viburnum bushes alongside her peach bungalow. She lived on a hill off a dirt road. Horace's house you couldn't see for the trees. She called him like she was calling a dog she was privately friendly with out of the woods. Horace and his mother had lived up there as long as Aunt Evelyn could remember.

"Horace!" she yelled. "Come on down here. I want you to meet young Westley."

Soon I heard a screen door slam.

"You hear?" Aunt Evy said. "He's coming. Talk to him like you might anybody, Uncle Ed, say."

Uncle Ed was always telling dirty stories. Then laughing so hard I'd join in, even though I couldn't quite understand. He told me he came home every day for lunch and laid Aunt Evelyn on the mohair sofa in their living room. After, he'd eat an egg sandwich and have his coffee. Do it in the nighttime, too, he said. Then begin laughing.

One story he told was when he was younger he'd broken his arm playing City League Softball, but that didn't stop him from still stabbing Aunt Evelyn on the sofa. Three days later during their matinee, he was trying to shift positions in the love act when he tumbled off the couch and broke his leg. That set him howling.

Ed was portly and not too bright like Aunt Evelyn said Horace was. "Horace can recite history better than any book you read in school," she said.

Aunt Evelyn, about five years ago, had started to flutter, vibrate. First it was her hands. Then over time we noticed it creep up her arms. Then her head. The head just sort of bobbed on the top of Evy's torso. Yet, Uncle Ed and her were still doin' it, close to twenty years now.

Well, when I saw Horace, he looked normal enough, excepting he was skinny and his arms moved independent of his mind. His hair was long, too. He looped down through the beech trees and under one arm were several composition books, and in the pocket of his shirt (his sleeves were rolled up above his elbows) ink pens and pencils were lined up. Looked like a dozen. He wore gold-rimmed glasses that were bottle-thick.

"This is my nephew Westley, Horace. He's a bright young boy. Like you Horace. He's also my dear friend, just like you, Horace. I told him you know more history than his school book. That you in truth know more dates and numbers and facts than any single book in the whole wide world! Ain't that right, Horace?"

Horace blushed and turned away, sounding an embarrassed chortle. He lifted his feet up and down on the grass rhythmically. It's then I spotted his right ear—it'd grown back into Horace's head like a bellybutton.

"Ask Horace a question, Westley."

We'd just been studying the Civil War in grade school. "General Sumpter," I said.

"General Sumpter?"

"Yes."

"His wife or his children? Their ages or their names? His house or its acreage? His battles, their dates, casualties—men or horses—or their rations?"

Evelyn interrupted. She could see Horace becoming more anguished, crimson was rising up into his face fast. It was as if he were about to explode in frustration. She told me later she was afraid he'd scream and begin running through their woods. Mrs. McCool would get upset with her.

"Westley, don't confuse Horace! The questions must be very precise. He will answer any of your history questions. But frame them precisely.

"How tall was General Sumpter, Horace?" she volunteered. "That's what the boy wants to know."

"Six feet four inches," came the rapid response with a grand sigh. Like the air coming out of one of Uncle Ed's tires on his sporty Ford coupe with the metal tire holder looking like a spoke wheel attached to its trunk.

"Was he handsome, Horace?"

"Very handsome, Ma'am. Blue eyes and soldierly bearing. Size twelve shoes and walked with a slight limp. Not a war injury. A farm implement injury—a harrow. His wife's name was Emma. They had twelve children, Sadie, Beatrice . . ."

At that point Aunt Evelyn again interrupted. "That's fine, Horace. You did very well." And Horace blushed again, going into his little tap routine on the grass, turning the knotted ear to both of us like a cyclopean eye. I sat down in the grass, Horace alongside me. He moved close.

"Are you my friend?" he asked.

"Yes," I answered after glancing up to Aunt Evelyn to see how I should respond.

"Fine," he said. "I like scholars."

Aunt Evelyn nodded.

Then told me she'd be down in the kitchen if I needed anything, leaving me there in the tall grass with Horace. "Two scholars" he kept repeating matter-of-factly like he was cementing sod in the earth, tamping it down to get a firm catch. Then he held out two pencils, a red one and blue one, asking me to take the one I wanted. He handed me a composition book. I opened it up and there were letters and numbers in very orderly columns but at random angles across each of its pages. The letter Q followed by a 3865, say, then a grouping of letters—some uppercase some lower with no definable pattern emerging, trailed by the numbers again. Nothing in any order apparent to me. No series of letters spelled a word—backward, forward, or jumbled—that I knew. But they were written with a most careful hand, like a scrivener's, page after page.

Periodically I'd find a blank page. As I leafed through the book, he watched me intently. I was careful to show no emotion. Finally I looked up to see if I could at least fathom some reason in his eyes for these hundreds and hundreds of columns, almost as if they were thin glass vials in which he had dropped a number, a series of letters, then more numbers, a letter and a number and so on to the vial's rim, then capped the cylinder to begin a new one. Test tube cylinders, perhaps. Page after page all in pencil.

Horace beamed when I looked at him. Immensely proud of what he had achieved. "This is magnificent, Horace."

We were sitting but his feet began to twitch as if they were shuffling that dance, that embarrassed dance again, and the belly-knot ear swung round to eye me like a search light.

"Westley," he said. "Only Horace can do this. Nobody in this whole wide world..." and he gestured back to his mother McCool's house and then to Aunt Evelyn's house, then off to the woods and the dirt street. "Only Horace McCool can do this. Come," he said, "I'll teach you." And he flipped open to one of the blank pages in my composition book. "I've saved that one for you," he said.

He opened his book to a fresh page.

"Just begin," he said. "First ...," he reflected and looked up into Aunt Evelyn's willow tree, "a ... G!" he cried.

I wrote a G.

"329810!" These came in a rush.

I columned these. He cast a critical eye over my work. I had written 32 under the G. This upset him. He erased it, wrote the 3 then the 2 under the 3.

"OK," he said.

And that's how we spent that afternoon in the grass. Writing random numbers and letters (apparently they weren't) into his "journals." Towards the end of our sessions, he looked exhausted.

"Are you tired?" I asked.

I could see the sun beginning to fall behind Aunt Evelyn's house. The sweat had gathered on both our bodies, and the flies were becoming pesky. Horace slapped at them, anguished, as if they were meddlesome children who wouldn't let us alone.

"Yes," he said, "very tired."

"Let's put the journals away for today, Horace."

"Yes, let's," he said. I gathered his pencil and mine, placed them back into his shirt pocket exactly in the order they came. I stood up, then reached down to lift him out of the tall grass.

He turned to walk slowly back toward Mother McCool's house. Like he was dead tired.

"I'll tell my class I met General Sumpter's historian in the woods today, Horace!" I hollered up to him. He turned his head so that I saw the deformed ear. Down in the grass where we had been sitting that long afternoon, it looked like a deer or a lion or perhaps a bear had napped. The day was drawing to a close. Shortly Uncle Ed would return home. The two of them would disappear into their darkened living room. The shades were always drawn when I walked through her house.

I could hear Uncle Ed laughing, talking sweet talk to Aunt Evelyn; her rejoinder would always be a gentle, "Come on, Ed, get on with it. Please."

I'd think about Klondike bars and General Sumpter and Horace with the bellybutton ear and Tony Prioletti's happy wake. Patrick McCart's unhappy one, and the spot in the field where the tall grass had been tamped down and where Horace and me sat . . . thinking somebody had laid there in the hot afternoon and the sun rolled down over Aunt Evelyn's hill and her hurrying Ed on and him chortling, riding her down into the old wire-spring sofa lunch time, dinner time, and Horace, up in his shuttered house with Mother McCool, building glass cylinders of random numbers and letters in column containers, some code that he understood, one ear already turned inward . . . . And I thought about the Joker and the Kings and Queens in Tony's casket, the games of chance and the ether-booze to smooth the edges of surprise.

Then I'd go back inside Aunt Evelyn's house when I'd hear her in the kitchen.

"Your Uncle Ed's taking a nap on the sofa," she'd remind. "We must be quiet. How did you like Horace?" she asked.

I looked out her window beyond the willow tree seeing the day die, and became afraid of the oncoming night. Watching Horace tiredly lope back through the trees toward home to the darkened Mother McCool's house, it all bubbling inside me sad . . . Christ, it all felt so hollow, like I was spinning away from earth . . . and I'd hear Uncle Ed snoring on the mohair sofa, and watch her bent over the stove in the darkening kitchen, fry pan of eggs all twirled together, her shaking, shuddering, her feet almost dancing like Horace's when he blushed.

I wanted it to stop.

"It's time for you to go home, Westley," she said. *Uh-huh*, I thought. I know. There are even stranger things you don't want me to see.

"OK," I answered. "I'll come back again soon, Aunt Evelyn. "Thanks for the wonderful day."

She'd nod just like Horace. Still stirring the eggs in the black skillet. Never looking up. Trembling, shuddering, the kitchen becoming darker by the minute. Her dance on the linoleum floor more agitated.

"Soon, Westley. Soon."

On my way home, as I walked through the shadowy streets of Hebron, I tried to think of Tony's funeral. How giddy everyone was. The big smile on his face. How he'd be playing golf somewhere now at twilight. Or sitting in his old garden shed in the sky playing cards with his cronies and drinking booze.

That night I dreamed about the battle of General Sumpter, but saw Horace, with his knotted ear, in cavalry attire. Behind him were all these medics carrying litters. Horses dragging litters. On these litters were columns of numbers and letters. But the columns were bent and twisted; they were broken. Single numbers and letters were falling, dripping on the battlefield's grass like blood. And General Horace's stony face, wounded, resigned, headed to the Mc-Cool house through the woods. In the background I could hear a dirge, a loud moaning sound, a mournful cry as if it rose out of the ground, and I looked up and saw General Horace McCool stop the procession, draw his left hand to cover his good ear, capping it.

Within days Mother met me at school. "Evelyn's dead," she said. I cried unashamedly on the schoolhouse steps. Sitting in the back seat of the old Dodge, I tried to envision happy things, and saw Uncle Ed passing out Klondike bars at the wake. To Horace and me, Mother and Father and all Evelyn's friends. And I tried to think of happy things in her casket. I saw a huge sunflower lifted from the back of her property lying next to her, casting its mustardy twilight on her cheeks. Her head no longer randomly shaking. And vials of colored water, violet, raspberry-red, and a sea-green, with ginger-brown stoppers, lying alongside her right hand. A kind of watery resurrection, the water of the streams in heaven, I thought . . . and the children eating Klondike bars smiling and saying goodbye to her and how we'd meet her up in the fields, up there next to Mrs. McCool's house, waiting for her to call the Horaces of this world to come out and play with us and take all our tears away.

To teach us the history of life. And just how goddamn blue General Sumpter's eyes really were.

"Goodbye, sweet Evelyn," I said. You knew his bellybutton ear would never startle me. How I'd think it looked like a strange exotic flower, really. You knew how I'd never embarrass you or him. The Horace to whom no one else in our family would you dare introduce.

"And you also knew how quickly afternoons come to an end. That the Uncles of this world would soon arrive home. That you'd have to undress. Not in the grass, but on the semen-encrusted, umber-wool sofa the two of you had bought on time twenty years earlier. Then after he shot, you'd stir up his eggs in the black skillet at dark."

# DAY LABORER

THERE ARE TIMES when depravity beckons each of us down. I was a day laborer in Pittsburgh. At 6:00 a.m. most days, I arrived at a store-front office on Grant Street to register, hoping to be summoned to the front desk. Occasionally there would be calls to send a man out to a house to help a missus weed, paint, or clean the attic, but most jobs were perniciously toxic or required a strong back. Sometimes an assignment would last a month or longer. I'd just come off a crew that scrubbed down the insides of empty oil tanks on a refinery outside the city. We crawled through a pipe coupling at the base of the tank into liquid amber shafts of cathedral, almost seraphic, light pouring through a hatch a dozen stories up— excepting it was like working inside a bottle of glycerin. Outfitted in rubber suits, we had to exit every five minutes for air.

Day laborers for the most part are drifters, ex-cons, and alcoholics, but generally gifted with a comedic self-awareness. Our tasks were simple enough in that they required no intelligence, and enterprising contractors were always available to capitalize on our cheap labor.

I couldn't smell a ripe peach for a month after the tank job. But I never refused an assignment, save one: painting a radio tower on Mt. Washington, Pittsburgh's highest peak. A corpulent, red-headed Irishman climbed out of a turquoise Cadillac one morning, and promising high pay, took several of us to the site for a demonstration.

The contractor situated one volunteer in a canvas bosun sling and by a winch and gas-driven motor hoisted the man up the side of the tower. I don't know how many stories he rose, but we could barely see the red light blinking on the tower's tip. Up the guy went until he looked like a damn bag of cats, and just then a terrific breeze came up and swung him pendulum-like out to one side of the radio tower then back again. Tick tock!

"Christ almighty," I cried. "He's gonna fall!" We could see the man struggling to hold onto the hawser.

"How in the fuck is he supposed to paint if he's ding-a-linging like that, mister?" another volunteer challenged.

"He hits it with a brush at each pass," the Irishman casually replied.

*Yeah, and fuck me,* I thought, walking back to my rooming house that day, poorer, but happy for another night's sleep.

\* \* \*

I'd been especially nice to Sam, the employment's office dispatcher, every few days "going for coffee." I'd slip a fiver into an empty cup which he'd then place into an open desk drawer. Later he'd look up at me and grin.

My first day back after the refinery detail, he motioned me forward. "Doyle, I got a job for you, if you think you want it."

"What is it, Sam?"

"Well, there's this widow over in Oakland by the university who always asks for Tommy Jessup." (Mr. Jessup was an unassuming, gentlemanly, middle-aged black man who always showed up early like me but dressed in a white shirt and tie.) "He goes out and works for her for a couple of days. Maybe she calls him twice a month. But Jessup ain't shown for some time. You interested?"

"What's Tommy do?"

Sam shrugged his shoulders. "Paints or gardens, maybe?" and handed me her address. The "widow" lived in one of the fanciest estates in all of Pittsburgh, located on the border of Oakland and Shadyside. (I lived a half-mile away in a run-down rooming house.)

It was the old brick and stone Hoyt estate that looked like a Moorish castle. Its grounds, bordered by a cast-iron spear fence, occupied an entire city block. I rang the buzzer at the gate.

"I'm here to see June Bauer."

"She's in 128 Columbine B, sir. Take a right at the end of the block and halfway up you'll see a pedestrian gate. Inside is the Bauers' residence."

I'd passed the wooded Hoyt estate countless times and never saw more than one residence. A huge carriage house sat alongside Columbine Road, but Edgar Hoyt stored his collection of antique Dusenberg's there. Yet, there sitting humbly under an oak tree, looking like a prefabricated World War II barracks, stood a metal Quonset hut. Alongside, an awning suspended from the hut to two poles served as a makeshift garage for a decade-old Chevrolet sedan. *It's one of the servant's quarters*, I thought.

I knocked.

"Come in."

It was exceptionally humid that day with no breeze. When I opened the door to 128 B, a rush of refrigerated air that had been vaporized with apple-scented perfume filled my lungs. Ah, no diesel fuel.

"Close the door!" a woman's voice snapped. But I could see no *she*. The interior was pitch black except for a black-and-white TV screen the size of a dime novel flickering halfway down the hut. I shut the door.

"Sit down."

But where? My eyes began to adjust to the darkness. She was to the left of me on a bed. About the hut lay an oscillating fan, a lawn mower missing one wheel, a pressure cooker, soiled plates, wine goblets and Dixie cups on every surface; there were milk crates and roller skates, a miniature apartment washing machine with crank wringers, a Christmas tree that had turned rusty brown, jury-rigged water pipe clothes racks draped with garments, and women's shoes—I couldn't walk but for tripping over a veritable history of shoe styles over the past two decades. The sepulcher voice spoke again.

"Sit down."

At the side of a rococo sleigh bed sat a half-upholstered Louis the Fifteenth chair draped with a floral evening dress. On its seat, a gold-rimmed dinner plate and denture soak set.

"Take that crap off that chair and sit down."

Mr. Green Jeans was singing "Old Macdonald Had a Farm" on the television.

"What's your name?"

"Peter Doyle."

"Where's Mr. Jessup?"

"Tommy hasn't been in for a couple of weeks. The man at the employment office sent me instead."

"Stand up and let me look at you."

I stood up.

"Turn around."

I obeyed.

"Sit down." She sighed and crawled down to the foot of the bed, flipping the dial to a quiz show.

The woman had white hair that had a Dynel texture and appeared to be in her late fifties, though I couldn't tell for certain. Parchment-skin white, gaunt but hardy, and dressed in a frilly nightgown, she sat propped up against one of those overstuffed bed chairs with arms. On a nightstand sat several empty beer bottles.

Under her bed covers and about her legs, I watched what looked like gophers tunneling under a lawn. The counterpane was suddenly riveting, alive with activity about her knees and bottom. But she paid the commotion no attention. Finally, a wire-haired terrier popped its head out from under the counterpane. Quickly followed by three others.

At least in the oil tank I knew what the hell was expected of me.

"I'm June Bauer," she said. "What's your name?"

"Peter Doyle."

"You a college boy?"

"A little school in West Virginia."

"Which one?"

"Waynesburg. You heard of it?"

She took a sudden quaff of beer, nodding. "What'd you study?"

"Philosophy and English."

"Mr. Jessup—he wasn't educated. You say he's sick?"

"Mr. Jessup hasn't reported to the office, that's all I know."

"You know anything about upholstering?"

"I covered a foot stool in wood shop once."

"I got a chair that needs re-upholstered?"

"Oh, but not professionally."

"Take that thing you're sitting on."

"But this chair is a fine antique, ma'am. It just needs to have the fabric cleaned."

"I don't like chintz." She jabbed the air in the direction of the manor house. "Reminds me of him. Tear the shit off of it."

"The wood is going to be raw and full of tack holes."

"Mr. Jessup's sick, you say?"

Finding any tools in the room would have been miraculous.

"Use a shoe for a hammer. Get a damn knife from the kitchen. Use your ingenuity."

Off to the side of her bed sat a small galley kitchen separated from the living area by an accordion door. I nearly fainted from the stench. It looked like an Edward Kienholz sculpture: half-eaten sandwiches waxed by gentian mold and soup plates of ash-gray gel crowded every surface. Flies and cockroaches were in abundance.

"Did you get a knife?"

I found one slathered with mayo on top of the refrigerator, wiped it clean on her curtains and set about ripping and prying the chintz off the chair's armrests. Mrs. Bauer now was deeply engrossed in *Queen For a Day*.

The money was easy. All I had to do was sit in an air-conditioned shed in the dark with my employer, watch TV and do *odd* jobs. When I'd finally stripped the arm rests of the fabric and jute stuffing and pried out the upholstery tacks with some difficulty, I asked, "Is this what you wanted?"

"I used to sit naked in that chair with my legs crossed waiting for the old bastard to fuck me. It didn't look any better even then," she said. "You hungry?"

"No."

"I'm famished. Fix me a sandwich. Turkey and tomatoes are in the fridge—and put mayonnaise on it. Make yourself one, too. But fetch me a bottle of beer first." She swept the empties off her side table. They chinked against others on the floor before rolling under the bed. The dogs stirred.

Unsure of what may jump out, I hesitated before opening the refrigerator door. It was now noon and, I presumed, oppressively hot outside. The terriers leapt out of her bed and bounded yapping into the kitchen. Oddly enough, the Frigidaire was the cleanest, most orderly spot in the residence. Bottles of beer stood upright and on their sides, like in a commissary, and in a butcher's paper package tied with string sat the luncheon meat. I found an overripe tomato on the sink board along with the jar of mayo.

"This mayonnaise should be refrigerated, Mrs. Bauer."

"Mr. Jessup's a lot smarter than you, boy! Will you make me the damn sandwich?"

I'd sat beside Tommy Jessup for many a morning at the employment office, shared cigarettes with him, laughed, and swapped day-laborer stories. But he hadn't ever told me about you, Mrs. Bauer.

\* \* \*

She shut off the tube with a jury-rigged switch up near her pillow. Only a sliver of daylight knifed the green opaque window blinds. A paler light bled under the door.

"Mr. Doyle. Are you a good judge of women's ages?"

"The illumination in here isn't so good, you know," I said.

A white-haired apparition now, the dogs devouring her sandwich at the foot of the bed, June Bauer brushed back her hair, holding an art-deco hand mirror to her face. From under her pillow she withdrew a powder puff and erratically dabbed her nose and cheeks; the cloud of talcum rose to the ceiling, nimbusing the bed. She painted kiss-my-ass magenta lips on her face—her mouth a sink hole in the sand whose sides threatened collapse.

"You think I'm forty-five, Mr. Doyle?"

"If I saw you in the daylight . . . perhaps. Can I ask you a question, Mrs. Bauer?"

"If it isn't too personal." She laughed and lit a cigarette.

*Emphysema.*

"Do you always lie in bed like this?"

"Is losing one's charm being handicapped, Mr. Doyle?"

The dogs leapt back up onto the bed and burrowed under the covers, settling themselves about her thighs. I began to perspire. She ruffled her nightgown top and sat up straight—her skeletal arms bearing down on the pillow chair.

"Do I attract you, Mr. Doyle?"

"You're an attractive woman, Mrs. Bauer." Earlier on the chiffonier in the room's far corner I spied several photographs of a much younger woman who looked uncannily like Grace Kelly.

"*Stop it!*" she yelled, smacking the dogs routing under her counterpane. The minuscule light caught dust shafts rising to the ceiling. Then she leaned toward me at such an angle that her breasts rolled gracefully out of her decolletage, glowing alabaster in the inky darkness. "*Do you consider these attractive, Mr. Doyle?*"

Do I reach out and cup them in my hands? Within moments I'd be lying next to her in the antique sleigh bed, shooing the terriers away. For there are no apparent boundaries in unilluminated grottos. The detritus of a materialistic civilization pebbling up about us. A comely woman once, requesting her day laborer's embrace. Now I understood what Mr. Jessup did.

I'd been hired out as a gigolo.

Furthermore, I would be recompensed for my services in a room so dark that I didn't have to see whatever I didn't wish to. Perhaps like the animals under the counterpane. June Bauer waited for me to cup her pearlescent fruit in the cleanest bowl in the potting shed—my perspiring hands. And end up like the rest of the shit on the floor.

"Yes," I said, "like porcelain in this cave. You must have taken great care to maintain them." I excused myself for a beer. Stoic Tommy Jessup. He got fucked *and* got paid. A nice turn of events for any day laborer.

It took each of us several minutes for our libidos to exhale the heat of her unrequited offering.

"Thank you, Mr. Doyle," she sighed. The woman, the proud one in the sepia photographs on the chiffonier, now turned to face me in the shadows. "Thank you for not taking advantage of me."

"It might have been fun," I lied.

"Perhaps," she said crisply. "Do you know who I am?"

I'd passed the estate for several years, often watching Edgar Hoyt leave for work in the morning with his chauffeur. But I'd never seen a lady about the premises . . . until today.

"I am Edgar Hoyt's wife."

I was stunned.

"Strange, don't you think?"

"Does he visit you *here*?"

"Oh, occasionally we pass each other in the driveway. But it is the briefest of encounters, for he chooses not to acknowledge my presence. Twenty years now."

"My God."

She lit another cigarette, offering me one. "Where are you from, Mr. Doyle?"

I leaned over the bed for a light. "A small town outside of Erie called Hebron."

"I'm from Michigan. I went to New York City as a young girl right out of high school. After a short period of playing bit parts on Broadway I got exceptionally lucky and became a Ziegfeld Girl. Sheer chance and some beauty, Mr. Doyle. Then Edgar Hoyt III, scion of Pittsburgh's barge and banking family, on one of his many pleasure trips East spotted me in the Follies and began chasing me. He's a very wealthy man, you know?"

Her pencilled eyebrows arched comically.

I sat back in the chair I'd stripped bare.

"Following a brief but tempestuous courtship and two ocean voyages to Europe, he asked me to return to Pittsburgh as his wife . . . to live in that *palazzo* over there."

"It's a magnificent estate, Mrs. Bauer."

"It's a mausoleum, Mr. Doyle. Edgar and I gave birth to a son in it. He's about your age in fact. I became *June Bauer Hoyt*, exemplary wife and hostess of the Hoyt dynasty. Dinner parties and public appearances galore—I was the *Ziegfeld Girl* in Pittsburgh! They'd been waiting for somebody to shine like a diamond in their damn soot."

She opened another beer. I sensed the sun had begun to fall in the sky. It was warmer inside the shed now. As if the air conditioning window units were tiring. Pleasant enough, but not chilled like the morning.

"But then Edgar became . . . well, strange. He'd place a towel under me when we made love. He got fussy about how I hung my clothes in our shared closets, chaffed about finding my body hairs in the bathtubs or in the sinks. Soon he insisted we sleep in twin beds. Finally he retired to a clinically clean room of his own on the uppermost floor—void of any furnishing save a monk's cot on a hardwood floor—and communicated to me solely through our servants. We never did engage in sex again. This once virile but gentle playboy within a span of three short years had grown into a cantankerous, crabbed, and obsessively fastidious prick; our marriage sunk from being Follies gay to Pittsburgh bleak.

"I checked into a sanatorium and upon my return home, the help ushered me here into their old planting shed sweet Edgar had refurbished in my absence. We remain husband and wife to this day."

The hum of the air conditioner now sounded intrusive.

"Well, what do you make of it, Mr. Doyle?"

"It must be very demeaning to you . . . and your son."

"Unlike you or Mr. Jessup, I've never really worked, Mr. Doyle. I was groomed to allure. To attract men like the white gardenia I am . . . *or was*. When I need companionship, I go to the local saloons after dark—or call your employment office. It's drafty over there in the *palazzo*, anyway." She swept her arm over the litter, mockingly triumphant. "But this is mine, Mr. Doyle. All fucking mine." Then eyeing me squarely—"*And I almost had you by your pecker, too, boy.*" She rolled her china breasts out before me once again.

"What other jobs do you have for me to do, Mrs. Bauer?" I asked, standing.

"You aren't doing what you're being paid for doing—sit down!"

It was time to leave.

"Authors!" she said, handing me a tablet and a pencil from her bed stand drawer. "Who are your favorites? Steinbeck, Fitzgerald? Write down their damn names and their best works. Philosophers, too—Nietzsche, Kant? No need to give me a synopsis, 'cause for an ignorant old Ziegfeld Girl, it'd all be gobbledegook anyway. To-morrow morning I'm going to call Kaufman's bookstore and have every damn one of them delivered."

She shot straight up in bed once again, fiercely shaking her sat-iny head like a Kabuki mistress. "Being you ain't at all interested in my ass, Mr. Doyle, perhaps I can *attract* you with my intellect?" Then she convulsively cackled and collapsed back under the bed covers, her pets repositioning themselves like rodents.

The doorbell rang.

"Answer it, please." Appearing shaken, she sat stiffly up in bed, blotting her lipstick on the bed sheet. The daylight and heat bar-reled into the roomful of litter. Evan Bauer stood on the threshold, a classmate of mine from Waynesburg.

"My God, Evan, what are you doing here?"

"Visiting my mother." He smiled. "And you?"

Gesturing that I leave the door open, he strode to the bed, leaned over and kissed June Bauer on the cheek with a cheerful "Hello!"

I was mortified.

The pair talked animatedly for several seconds. Then Evan turned. "Mother says you've been a real gentleman, Doyle. It's nice of you to help out." He shook my hand warmly. "Make sure she pays you a just wage, even if all the money's stashed over there in Edgar's castle." They both laughed as he departed.

"You knew," I said.

"I didn't expect Evan today," she replied. "I apologize if his see-ing us together embarrassed you."

"Oh, no," I said. "We weren't close friends." *Did he think I'd slept with his mother?* Evan's face betrayed no emotion other than the bonhomie of a good son. He maneuvered our Scylla and Charybdis masterfully.

"Where will he go now?" I asked.

"Next door to pay respects to his father—and gather money."

I rose to leave.

"Do you know what I do when I get real hard up for men, Mr. Doyle?"

The television set began flickering again. I moved toward the door.

"No," I said, standing soberly in the corner.

"I put brown sugar between my legs and make them lick it off."

The light from the opening door slowly illuminated her bitter grin, then the audition photographs on the chiffonier.

"It's an old Ziegfeld trick, Mr. Doyle. How much do I owe you?"

"Nothing," I replied.

"The envelope's on your day's work," she said flatly.

A manila pay envelope stuffed with one-dollar bills sat on the chair I'd desecrated. *You stash envelopes under your pillow for Tommy*, I thought.

"I paid you for two days," she explained. "Just like I always do him—excepting I'll not be needing your services tomorrow, Mr. Doyle. Edgar and I don't expect the help to work on the Sabbath. We walk our dogs instead."

# *THE SCAR*

## I

THE POST OFFICE Café was where our old man hung out on Saturday morning. Westley and I thought he'd be lubricated enough by noon to answer our genealogical questions. Regaling several of his drinking buddies and Grace, the bartender, with ribald wit, Father greeted us amiably. His friends suggested we were damn near old enough to drink the old man under the table.

But drinking held no attraction for either of us.

"Pap, we got a few questions for you."

"Yeah. Sure. Where you going? You need some money?"

"No. We're fine." Westley was frank and direct with the old man. "Pap, Ma said we could go visit Grandma and Grandpa Coleridge if we wanted."

"You shitting me?"

"It's for real. Sort of like a history lesson. What's the rest of them like?"

He lost his color, then uttered darkly, "*Vipers.*"

"Don't bullshit us, Pap." Westley tried to humor him.

"See for yourself." He turned back to the bar.

"They can't be that bad," I said.

"Let me tell you both something," he guided us off our chromium bar stools and led us into the back of the café, where several pinball machines were lined up against one wall, casting a curious yellow-and-blue glow on our faces. "Those people down there in sheep-shit hollow mean nothing but trouble. Why in Christ's name do you think we never told you about them? Why don't we carve the goddamn turkey with either her family or mine, or knock on their doors at Christmas?

"They're trouble, that's why. Particularly your mother's brood. Crepe hangers, malingerers, thieves, convicts, bill jumpers, whores, and worst of all, downright snake-mean. Knock on their fucking doors all you want, but cry out you ain't a couple of bill collectors, or they'll shoot the baby balls off both your asses sooner than look at you."

He escorted us back up the aisle of the café, took the several dollars of change he had lying on the counter next to his glass of beer and shot tumbler, stuffed the bills in my shirt pocket, and feigned a hearty farewell, lying so everybody could hear him: "Enjoy the ball game, Sons! Mahoning Township over Nashanock by three runs. We'll split the winnings!"

\* \* \*

A tiny movie theatre, several ladies' stores, one men's shop featuring a Dizzy Gillespie cutout, a hair salon, and a McGory's five-and-ten clustered at the heart of Long Avenue; farther along, sorry bungalows hugged its curbs clear to the horizon. Just beyond the commercial section stood the Methodist AME, a modest wood-frame building with a gabled slate roof and a shingled turret out of whose tip rose a gold-leaf cross, one which Jake Daugherty, Pap's father, maintained. The church's display case, enclosed by a glass door, announced in white plastic letters, "*Death, Where Be Thy Sting?* by Samuel Hochner, Rev." Less than a city block down the street, a similar Regent Theatre display case read, "*On A Wing And A Prayer.*" The price for admission was so inexpensive it mattered little to most patrons what was playing.

Pennsylvania Avenue ran perpendicular off Long Avenue. A single-story Baptist church sitting on one corner suggested its parishioners were less well-off than Reverend Hochner's flock up on

Long Avenue. In fact, the farther away you journeyed from He-bron's Diamond, the less grand and monumental the houses of worship became. This Baptist sanctuary looked as if it could have been a mechanic's garage but for its lime-white doors, the celluloid purple paper adorning its windows, and a makeshift crucifix nailed up against the eaves over the doorway. It, too, had a bulletin board, but this was a simple affair hanging off a hook at the entrance, with a paper tacked to it broadcasting, "*Sin and Mary's Burden*, Preach-er Billy Leech. Pancakes & Sausage Following."

Across the street a creek rippled out of a culvert and spread a car-length's wide to flow alongside Pennsylvania Avenue, which by now had turned to gravel. Beyond the stream and to our left stood a Federalist mansion on a rise overlooking the swift and brackish water. No visible bridge crossing or roadway led into this house, once quite magnificent, but now with several of its upstairs win-dows gone, and gauze curtains flying out over the porch roof.

Shoeless children attired only in underpants raced sinisterly in and out of the house, its door wide open to a black interior. Two teenage girls (we guessed they were all siblings) ran down to the water's edge, taunting Westley and me to join them. The oldest, boyishly gaunt, flashed an obscenity while provocatively snapping her sister's dress above her head—she was stark naked.

"Do you suppose that's 1648?" Westley asked.

The address we were seeking stood directly across the street, a white clapboard-sided bungalow with a small front porch and a suggestion of a second story. A 1932 Chevrolet Coupe sedan sat in its driveway.

"Are you sure *this* is the place?" I asked.

"If it ain't, we got nothing to worry about. You go first," Westley said. "You're the oldest."

"What are we going to say? 'Hi! We're the Daugherty boys'?"

"How about, 'Hello, we're your grandsons.'"

"What if they . . . I mean what in the hell *will* we call them if they let us in?"

"Maybe we should just go home," Westley said.

I pushed him up the porch stairs and knocked. Soon a curtain in the window of the door levitated, baring a pair of nut-brown eyes. Dumb, we stood looking down at our cheap shoes. Then I wondered if we should take the old man's admonishment seriously, and blurted out:

"*Do you think Grandma and Grandpa are home, brother Westley?*"

Westley began to laugh uncontrollably, like when he farted in church. The main door squeaked open. On the other side of the storm door stood a heavy-set girl of serious mien.

"Whadya want?"

"The Daugherty boys," Westley piped up like it was something to be proud of.

"What?" she yelled.

"The Daugherty boys. Katherine and Joe's sons."

"Oh." And she just stood there, gaping, delight now spreading like a red shadow across her moon face. "You mean Westley and James?"

Our mouths both dropped.

"Yes!" I answered happily.

"I'm Jenny," she said, opening the door wide. "We're cousins. Come on in."

A gold-leaf framed daguerreotype of a black horse stalking a white horse faced us as we entered the room. The white horse slanted her neck back towards the pursuing stallion with an air of submission. Crocheted antimacassars lay draped over the backs of a mohair sofa and chairs, upholstered in a soot-black and umber geometric pattern. Floor lamps sat on opposite ends of the sofa, orange marble and brass affairs with grand silk canopy-like shades many sizes too large. Miniature light bulbs underneath the marbled inlaid bases of these lamps provided the scarce illumination in the living room. The blind and drapes on the single window had been drawn closed.

On out into the kitchen we shadowed Jenny.

A gray-haired lady in a chemise, her neck jeweled by a large silver and pearl brooch, sat next to a table and bank of windows through which shafts of a pollen-filled sunlight swirled. A butcher's apron stopped short of her hosiery, garter-rolled just under her knees. I saw and smelled flour on her large hands and beefy arms, on her jowled cheeks and about her mouth where it powdered a mustache. Flour dust fogged the glass cupboards. It lay a thin film across the table and chairs and linoleum floor. It splotched her felt slippers like baker's rain.

"Grandma," Jenny exclaimed, "these are Aunt Katy's sons!"

The old woman supported her heavy body with her hands against the oaken table, stood up and shambled across the floor toward us, great handfuls of flesh hanging off her triceps. A flour-pocked, safety-pin-secured eminence slipping toward Westley and me, this flour lady, this massive maternal gathering of bone and flesh sliding her diabetic body across the linoleum to an embrace.

And we were sorely ashamed.

She pressed each of our heads to her breasts; they radiated a tantalizing odor that she left behind on every chair in which she sat. Even after she died, her odor lingered on the walls and chairs of that house for years. We'd been held by women before, but this woman gave off an odor like earth after winter thaw. A distinct, unwomanly odor. No sex here. On Katy Daugherty we could detect a variety of scents that came out of peculiarly colored bottles on top of her bureau. (Out of the ink-blue vial, one so provocative it caused me to experience a profound sense of loss when she dabbed it behind her ears.) But this massive sliding soul was a sweetness at the edge of sour.

And as she wept, clutching our heads like Mason jars confining fireflies and dandelions against her fleshy breasts, we began to melt before cousin Jenny. The brave Daugherty boys, whose father's sister was a burlesque queen, whose brother was a circus tramp, whose younger brother was a pious, mean-spirited, selfish-prick Monsignor of the old man's once-a-Catholic-always-a-Catholic Church.

I looked down at my hands, as she didn't seem to want to let go for a while longer. They, too, looked splotched as if by rain. Under a woodshed in a summer storm. In this place. The taunting girls with no clothes under their dresses across the creek could by no worldly means draw us away.

What in Christ's name could ever have gone so wrong?

## II

Myra Coleridge took Westley and me by the hand and walked us toward the back door out into her stockade-fence-enclosed backyard.

"Jenny, take the boys out to meet Grandpa."

"Oh, Gramps, come on out here!" Jenny ran towards the garage.

Several dogs leapt barking out of the garage and raced towards us. Grandma stamped her slippered foot against the stone path. The animals darted under the rabbit hutches, panting and wagging their tails. Everything became quiet.

Rupert Coleridge stepped into the afternoon light.

He walked deliberately over to the chicken house, tossing two handfuls of corn onto the hard earthen floor. Out of the miniature gabled-roof and columned-porch house several brilliantly feathered cocks strutted. He turned to study us.

A body of slight stature dressed in black, high shoes, a pair of gray woolen trousers held tightly up against his crotch by button suspenders over a matching short-sleeve shirt whose single breast pocket displayed several fountain pens fastened tightly against his chest. He wore a leather bow tie, too. A costume worn by a mortician's helper, the man who chauffeured old Packard hearses with the remaining dowagers through the center of Hebron.

Grandpa Rupert's head was small, with concave cheeks and deep-set onyx eyes, like windows under eaves. Bushy zinc-colored eyebrows. Like Jacob Daugherty, his hair was untamed and parted down the middle. But unlike Jacob, Rupert Coleridge had one outstanding distinguishing characteristic. Even from where Westley and I stood, it was painfully evident: a scar the width of a strip of bacon etched his forehead. It showed jaundiced in the sun, as if somebody once had taken a razor-sharp chisel and lifted off Rupert's bony forehead a flesh shaving, then ineptly stitched that strip of skin-bacon onto the left side of his nose.

For that is where in Jesus's name it wound up.

Half of Grandpa's nose came off his forehead. It, too, was a sick, mustardy hue. We could hear him sucking air forcefully through his nostrils from where we stood, almost snorting, same as the pony that stood roped in the shed next to the rabbit hutches. When we got close enough to him, the prosthetic half-nose would get some color in the yellow when he snorted forcefully—like red in a dying ochre sky.

"Pap, these are Katherine's boys."

"Oh?"

Pulling air up into his head, he reached out his right hand. On its back side was yet another scar like the one on his forehead. The hand was grease stained, and after seeing it, he withdrew it, commenting: "After all these years Katy don't want me to send her boys home dirty." He stopped at the rooster pen.

Jenny ran into the garage and returned with a coffee can full of seed corn. He poured us each a handful. The roosters had returned to their miniature house. Grandpa Rupert sounded chicken noises as he gestured for us to toss the corn into their enclosure.

"My babies. You boys know what these are?"

"Chickens," offered Westley.

"Chickens you eat," he scolded. "Whadayer names?"

"He's James. I'm Westley."

"I once seen you when you were babies. Didn't even know your names."

Both of us fidgeted.

"On a hot summer Friday night these chickens take in more money than your daddy do in a week. *Cocks*, boys. *Fighting cocks*. Each one of them is a killer."

He led us into his garage. A 1938 Plymouth convertible coupe with a rumble seat stood wheel-less on blocks. Its top was down and the single seat had been re-upholstered in a glossy green imitation leather. The garage's only source of illumination was a single small window looking back toward the kitchen; a trouble light still burned under the car's chassis. Near the driver's door lay a board onto which he'd bolted a pair of roller skates.

"I bet both of you boys would like to drive her, huh?"

A pair of fender skirts with emblems of silver comets and red reflector eyes lay against the garage wall.

"What are you doing with it?" I asked.

"Its transmission's shot. You boys know anything about cars?"

We didn't.

"Your daddy ain't taught you how to fix cars?"

"No sir."

"What do you do when yours gets broke?"

"He takes it to the gas station," Westley said.

"Costs money, huh?"

We shrugged our shoulders.

"Can't afford that down here on Pennsylvania Avenue. Rabbits just ain't for Easter, you know. Taste a lot like chicken." He slid under the Plymouth on the roller skates. "We fix what goes broke."

Westley and I stood in the dark staring at each other.

"How old are you, James?"

"Near sixteen."

"What's your daddy been teaching you?"

It was now becoming more uncomfortable in the dark and gasoline-impregnated interior. Periodically Grandfather Rupert would skate out from under the coupe on his back, retrieving another wrench out of the many buckets of tools he kept about the car's periphery, then disappear again.

"Oh, I don't know," I said.

"I seen him, you know?" He skated out once again, lifted his head in the glow of the trouble light and spoke: "Damn near every Friday night up at Keefe's Café in Hebron. He ever tell you?"

Both of us shook our heads.

"Always seems to be with one of his chickens."

He slid back under the chassis, chortling. He clanged one of his crescent wrenches against the transmission housing, for it sounded like the starting bell for the cock fight, then rolled triumphantly out from under the convertible, smiling widely at us in the darkness, reaching out both his hands to us, the scarred one and the one that weren't scarred, and beckoning us to lift him off the litter.

"Look here, boys," his coal-black eyes glinting under the bony eaves of his forehead, "I don't mean no disrespect to your father. I just ain't ever stomached how he's been treating your ma. Your old man strutting around downtown Hebron like he were one of those sportin' bankers on the North Hill, fancy layin' rags and shoes and spendin' all his money on women and drink . . . . Well, it just been cankerin' away in my stomach.

"But they"—he gestured toward the house—"ain't ever permitted me to speak." Grandpa put his bony arms about each our waists. I stood almost a head taller than both him and Westley. We walked back towards the house. At the kitchen he stopped and lifted a black leather change purse out of his trouser pocket, snapped it open and withdrew a roll of currency secured by a rubber band, peeling off ten one-dollar bills to each of us.

*"Welcome home."*

He placed his soiled hands on each our heads. The hands felt dry, bony, tightly wrapped, unlike Grandmother's, but nevertheless alive, and I could feel the grease-stained palm prints on my cheeks. A proud scar that I would infuse with crimson as Westley and I walked back to our house, miles away, never bothering to spend our ten one-dollar bills. Holding them in our pockets, smelling of gasoline and crankcase oil, and the sour-sweet odor of Grandma's flour embrace—carrying these odors and chimera back to our house, place of marital barrenness, whose mystery or death we never fully understood.

But now at least each of us had a place to which we could repair.

### III

We didn't have a garage like Grandpa Coleridge's. Ours contained a sofa whose springs had exploded, a rusted wringer washer and a Westinghouse mangle. An oak porch swing lay in its center, the eye hooks having pulled out of the decaying porch rafters one summer day when Mother and ailing Aunt Evelyn swung a late afternoon, watching the traffic race up and down Cascade street. When the swing collapsed, plummeting the two sisters to the porch floor, their legs shot out before them like wooden pegs. The cars continued to whiz past.

Evelyn began to laugh, exclaiming, "Katy. My goddamn swing's broken, too."

"Nonsense," Mother replied. "He didn't screw big enough ones in. If I'd done it in the first place, we wouldn't be sitting here on our sweet ones now. Let's hang the goddamn thing back up, set a cold beer on it, and wait 'til he comes home. Seein' him fly ass over tin cups in his fancy duds, it'd be worth it, wouldn't you say, Evy?"

Aunt Evelyn was now on her feet, trembling. "Oh, I wouldn't want to see him get hurt."

"Hurt!" Mother humphed, dragging the swing down off the steps and across the lawn towards the garage.

* * *

The black lacquered rocking chair with its cornflower stencils leaning to one side in its dark corner, for instance. That was the most telling symbol for her of how things had gone awry. It sat out there crippled for several years. One day I saw her dragging it toward our neighbors, Johnny and Mary Wazlinski. "If Johnny can repair it, it's yours, Mary," she said. Johnny, a welder's apprentice, took a scrap half-inch steel rod, heating it with a torch so it curved into the shape of a rocker, then welded two brackets down into which the chair's legs could sit. He sprayed the rocking contraption flat black. It worked fine, but much noisier now, and cut a trough in Mary's hardwood floor. She lay a piece of heavy carpet under it, claiming the Windsor rocker was the nicest piece of furniture she'd ever owned.

"Mother, what do you think of it?" I asked in private.

"Johnny fixed it for her. Ain't what your father did." Then added, "But it does look like a chair with a prosthesis."

When the old man finally saw it several days later, he said, "Maybe you should've had Johnny fix your rocker years earlier,

Katherine. 'Cepting you'd have to sew it a skirt to cover that nasty leg."

"It looks far better with Mary sitting rockin' in it than it did out there with the hubcaps and the Westinghouse."

"Katherine, if I'd jury-rigged a leg up like that and brought it in here, why, you know what you would have done?"

"You've ain't never given me a chance, Joe Daugherty."

She was right. He'd astonish her now and then. But his surprises were ones she always feared he might spring on her.

\* \* \*

"Boys, don't let on to your mother I'm telling you this." Father had huddled us down in the cellar out of Mother's earshot one dusk shortly after our south side visit.

"The old bastard is a *convict*," he whispered.

"A convict!" blurted Westley.

"Shhhh. Sweet Grandad. Did you like that big scar on his forehead? That nose that looks like a change purse patched with a piece of leather? How the old bastard snorts up through it, his left eye twitching like a warning light? He's some piece, ain't he?"

Neither of us said a word.

"Well, you think what you want about him. What'd he do? Pay you both off? Don't go in any of the stores on the south side sayin' you're related to old Rupert and Myra Coleridge; the proprietor will chase both your asses back out onto the street. That little banshee's a certified convict: *Leavenworth Federal Penitentiary*."

"What are you telling us?" I asked.

"Daddy Rupert had to leave town, go 'down south,' for several years to have his nose taken care of." He laughed sardonically when he saw we were reading him. "Well, that ain't the truth. Your ma's old man worked for the Baltimore and Ohio Railroad. Right down in the freight yards in Mahoningtown near the roundhouse, he and your grandmother's sister's husband, George, both switchmen. They hitched up a scheme one night. Several boxcars of goods they'd eased over to the rail siding alongside a fence borderin' the freight yards. Had their accomplices pull up on the outside of the fence after midnight with several dump trucks idling, while George and Rupert unsealed the two boxcars and threw all the freight stored inside over the fence to their accomplices. They worked through the night. Come daylight, the boxcars were broom clean.

"Dime store notions, kitchen utensils, pots and pans, dry goods, and a rich load of liquor—damn near half a boxcar's worth. The thieves all met the next day in a deserted warehouse to fence the loot, but old Rupert banjo-eyed one lot of black suits and men's dress shoes.

"That's just how the little snortin' sonofabitch got caught."

The pony mocked Grandpa's snorting in its shed that day, too.

"The black shoes looked like the kind bankers wore, huh, plain but with rich-looking leather laces? The suits were all one size, as were the shit kickers. Old Rupert took one set of clothes for himself, then had cousin Jenny walk up and down Pennsylvania Avenue gifting the remainder, explainin' to the Mrs. of the house: '*Pap Coleridge won a couple of suits with shoes in a contest in a raffle over at Lima, Ohio. A little of your tailoring, and maybe the mister would like it free?*' But the next Sabbath, Grandaddy, along with several of his neighbors, promenaded Pennsylvania Avenue wearing the purloined black suits and banker's shoes like low-water dignitaries, and walking back from the Baptist church just up the street, they got caught in an unexpected downpour. The black suit jackets held up just fine; but the pants lost their body and clung like shit-paper to the men's knees and thighs. Worse, the soles peeled right off their fancy banker's shoes like box tops.

"Grandpa Rupert and Uncle George were nabbed cold.

"*Corpse wrappers*, clothes undertakers dress stiffs in. The dress jacket had to be real. But the pants? Good enough if the widow looked under the tufted satin to ascertain her deceased was wearing trousers. Who gave a shit they were paper? But the items of clothing that put your grandfather and mother's uncle in the cooler were the fucking *cardboard-soled shoes*."

Katy began rattling the supper dishes overhead.

Pap wasn't about to break his rhythm. "When the drenched neighbors finally got into their houses, their shoe uppers were still tied and intact but the soles and heels had dropped somewhere between their homes and the Baptist church. *Hebron Chronicle* reported next day that nine pairs of cadaver shoes were among the loot. '*The dead don't walk*,' one of Rupert's benefactor's swore.

"A federal crime to steal from the railroads, boys."

"James! Come upstairs to wash up. Westley . . ." Mother called.

Father lowered his voice to a whisper. "Jail doctors discovered his nose cancer and cut the bad part away like you'd scoop rot from a peach, then shaved off a piece of his forehead to create his change-purse sniffer. Your mother's always been lied to that her old man was recuperating in a St. Louis hospital.

"The little banshee convict of Pennsylvania Avenue's a mean 'n sneaky little prick. That smile that he's giving you is as phony as those cadaver skins."

\* \* \*

By now night had penetrated the cellar. Only the streetlight cast an ochre blade across our old man's face. He seemed proud he'd driven his story home. Westley and me stayed seated while Father went outside and rolled his 1936 Dodge sedan out of the driveway. In the blackness we dreamed of a banshee convict roller skating under the chassis of ours.

# POPEYE'S DEAD

## I

*T*HE BAZAAR. INSIDE there it will all make sense. And my brother and I waited until both parents had fallen asleep, and drifted the car out of the driveway and down the street until it swung around the block, then I shoved it in gear and it kicked on; it began to hum, and we drove it deep into the night toward the lights we saw in the sky, the reflections, the illumination of the bazaar outside of town.

"Do you have any money?" I asked.

No. He had no money. And he sat sort of stiff but wide-eyed with one hand on the chromium door handle.

"It doesn't matter anyway. We don't need any money. If you get hungry, I'll get you something to eat. Just don't worry, OK? I see you sitting over there worrying. Well, don't worry. Do you hear? Don't worry."

I had grown tired of waiting. Waiting. And I had also grown tired of listening to him asking for me to take him for a ride. Hanging around. Waiting for me. But I was waiting. And not a goddamned thing seemed to ever move in that house. Was somebody going to take us on this trip? Or weren't they? And it didn't seem to be going to happen.

Well, I would. And in a ball field way outside town, they were parking the cars. Beyond the cars were the tents and the hundred lights. And he and I pulled the old man's car over by second base and walked toward the tents. He was about a foot smaller than me, but I had loaned him my leather jacket. It made him look older. But his fucking pants were too short. You could see if you looked down at his legs and shoes that he was still a kid. I mean a real kid. But he wasn't acting like a kid this night. And the two of us silently, no talking between us, continued walking, and at the gate we were greeted by a woman.

"Good evening, men," she said.

My brother nodded seriously, as if he had been here before.

"Where is your money?" she inquired.

"We haven't any," I said.

"Well, you have to have money to come in here. Gentlemen.

"Did you leave your wallets at home?"

My brother nodded seriously again.

She laughed out loud. "I can't imagine such gentlemen being without their wallets.

"Where do you keep your rubber jimmys? And the Popeye and Olive dirty pictures?

"You," she said, "the little one. I'm speaking to you."

And my brother looked straight ahead seriously. "Popeye's dead," he said.

"Popeye's dead!" And she laughed even more animatedly. Then reached down and cupped her hand at my brother's crotch, then squeezed. "How long has Popeye been dead?" she whispered.

"Popeye's been dead 100 years," he answered looking straight ahead, seriously. "Popeye died intestate. Olive's living on a poor farm over in Sharon. And my brother and I just come down here to spend the day. We're the Slatterlys."

She looked up at me still holding onto his little cock and remarked, seriously, "This one seems to know something that you or I don't, brother."

"Mr. Slatterly," she addressed him, still holding tight, "You ever been to such a place as this before?"

"No, I ain't. Just the state fair."

"Well, this ain't a state fair, Sir."

"I suspected it weren't," he answered.

"When did you begin to suspect that?"

"Well, when I looked up there and saw the sign."

"What sign?" She looked puzzled.

"The sign that says MIDGETS AND FREAKS GET IN FREE. Me and him's a midget and a freak. And I suspect you've already decided that, ain't you?" And he took her hand away from his crotch, began shaking it and saying, "Slatterly's the name. Jim Slatterly. Pleased to make your acquaintance."

And she let us in.

"Rubber jimmys and Popeye," he scoffed. "What she think we are? Kids?"

Neither of us seemed as self-conscious now that we had gotten in. And on either side of us for perhaps the length of a city block were tents with different colored lights decorating them. And men. Everywhere, men walking up and down the midway.

"Wouldn't it be a joke if we met the old man here?" he remarked.

I agreed. "Remember, we stick together here," I said. But despite his seeming nonchalance, I knew he wasn't about to run off. He'd stick close by, very close by. In front of each of the tents somebody stood on a wooden crate telling a story. Up and down the midway there were all these different men on boxes telling some story. And the flaps to each of these tents were drawn closed. Some tents had numerous men listening to the speakers; others had none, or virtually none. We were drawn to the tent with the greatest number of spectators. Jim pulled me right up to the front.

It seems we had just come in about the middle of the man's story. I couldn't quite make it out. It seemed all fucked up. Confused. The guy was talking seriously, just like a preacher, but everything was fucked up in the story. It made no sense to me. Something about an allegory and men in a cave and shadows and fire and Pluto, I thought he said. But my brother began laughing like hell.

"What's he saying, Jim? I don't understand a goddamn thing he is saying."

"I don't either," he said. "But you have to pretend you understand, or we'll get our asses kicked out of here."

So the both of us laughed. And laughed. And the speaker seemed to brighten up. And he pulled me up onto his box.

"This man here knows what I am talking about. Don't you, Sir? Now in your words, tell those men out there what I am trying to say. Tell them just what they are going to see once inside this tent."

My brother stood happily in front, urging me to speak. He cupped his prick with his left hand as if it were a signal, and nodded for me to speak.

"Well, you are talking about why we shouldn't hold our little lights under a basket."

"That's right!" he exclaimed. "Now tell them why."

"Because," I said, "Theology is the Queen of Science and she refuses, absolutely (I was feeling more courageous), to grab hold of any man's prick who doesn't believe in the Word of God, if you get what I mean."

"*Agape!*" I heard someone shout in the crowd.

"Bullshit," another rejoined.

"And you, little one," he motioned to my brother. "Have you anything to add?

"What's his name?" he asked me.

"Dan," I replied.

"You, Dan, what do you have to tell these men?

"Come on. Speak up. Don't be shy!" the speaker exhorted.

"Popeye's dead."

And the crowd of men began laughing. Like one body. Laughing hilariously. And my brother began laughing. Encouraged, he jumped up on the box with the speaker and me.

"Listen!" he shouted.

"You don't believe it?"

They became silent.

They expectantly waited for him to tell them more.

"Popeye's Dead," he said. And they resumed laughing. It was the way he said it. "Popeye's Dead. Popeye's Dead." It struck them all as being very funny. And he began jumping up and down on the box exclaiming "Popeye's Dead. Popeye's Dead. Popeye's Dead."

And by now the men had begun bending over in pain from intense laughter. Some had begun to roll on the ground. The speaker seemed perplexed. I, embarrassed. And my brother had no idea why they were laughing. He just presumed he was very funny.

And I grabbed him by the arm and told him we better get the hell away from this tent. Reluctantly he followed.

One of the spectators stopped us before we had found our way out of this particular crowd.

"My name is Eckersley," he said. "William Eckersley. I wonder if you two would follow me to my car?"

"What the hell for?" Jim asked.

"I have some books out there I think you might be interested in."

"What kind of books?"

And my brother gave me a look like—what in the hell was going on here? Strange ducks here.

"The *Gilgemesh Epic* for one. Have you ever heard of it?"

"Yeah," Jim answered. "We heard of it."

"Well, I got that for you and a book called *The Miller's Tale*. You heard of that, too?" he asked.

"Oh yeah," Jim answered. "But since Popeye's Dead we aren't going to buy dirty books anymore. Do you understand?"

The man seemed perplexed.

"It ain't got anything to do with you mister It's just that when poor Popeye Died we just throwed our dirty books into the box with him. And buried it all—Popeye and the books. Just wouldn't be right, you know. I mean continuing to read such books with Popeye being Dead.

"You know that saying about becoming a man and putting away childish things, Mr. Eckersley? Well, him and me—well him and me's just out here tonight breaking in our new shoes; and anyway the light's too dark for reading." And we walked away.

"That guy was a fairy, Tom. Furthermore, I ain't ever heard of those books. Probably some more Jiggs and Maggie. What the hell is it with these people? What do they think, we're stupid? Fuck them."

Jiggs and Maggie and Dr. Pangloss.

The optometrist across from Terminal Lunch. Perhaps we'd run into him here, too.

"Where in the hell are the women?" inquired my brother.

"I think that is what is inside the tents. The women are all in there."

"How do we get inside one?"

Time, I said. Just a matter of time. He had become restless now. He didn't want to hear anymore talk. No more lectures. No more words, speeches, diatribes, con-game spiels. He just wanted to see the women. Inside the many tents.

## II

"You boys interested in women?"

No one was in front of this tent. We hesitated. The speaker motioned us over.

*Why not*, I thought. That's what the hell I brought him here for. Why not get it done and over with, I reasoned. I had heard one speaker in a thick German accent mention Superman; and I thought we might want to go there.

But that would have to wait. The ticket taker by grabbing his little prick must have put the pox on him. No time or patience for inquiry now.

"Yeah. We're interested in women. What do you have?" he says.

The speaker, a man really not too much larger than my brother, wearing a mustache and a three-piece suit and black patent leather shoes and a chesterfield coat, he smiled. "All kinds of women," he replied. "Just what did you gentlemen have in mind?"

## III

That was a very difficult question to answer.

What kind of women did he have for a midget and a freak, I wondered?

"Speak up, Shorty. You don't want to keep them waiting, do you?"

I began laughing. What the hell could Jim say? He was either going to ask for the Virgin Mary or Olive. These being the only women he by any stretch of the imagination knew. I once caught him behind the bushes with my BB gun, the Winchester, pointing at the next door neighbor girl, about his age, and commanding her to dance or else he was going to shoot. But she had her clothes on. So I was indeed curious just what he would say.

"I want a woman whose tits are so sharp that she has to put band-aids over the nipples so as they won't cut through her sweaters."

"OK," said the man, pulling out a little 5-cent tablet, writing down my brother's orders. "Anything else?" he inquired.

"Yeah." He had his hands in his pockets now and was rocking back and forth on his little shoes like some business man. "I want her to have a big rosy belly that hangs out over her lace panties."

"Yes, sir," and continued writing.

"And between her legs..." he paused. The note taker paused. We all sort of waiting for this one.

"And between her legs..." he looked up at me briefly, "I would like to see Shirley Temple curls."

Nonplussed, the speaker looked at him.

"And inside these Shirley Temple curls I want a hole."

"What kind of a hole?" the man in the chesterfield inquired.

"About this size." And he made a ring with his thumb and his index finger. I'd say a 2 millimeter hole.

"That's a very small hole," the man protested. But noted that also. "Now what do you want inside that hole?"

This was a hard one. I wouldn't have been able to answer it.

"Well," he waxed, "I just want it hot inside there. It's got to be very hot."

"How hot?"

"Well, so hot that when I put my prick in the hole, I got to keep pulling it out and putting it in so fast because of the heat."

"But why can't you just put your prick inside the hole and leave it there?" inquired the man.

"That's how hot it's got to be, buddy!" he remonstrated.

"OK. I think I'm beginning to get the idea. Now is there anything else she's got to have?"

"One more thing," said Jim. "Make sure she is in heat."

"I don't understand."

"Well, goddamnit, I just don't want her eatin' an apple or something when I'm parting those curls and puttin' the prick in the hole. You get what I mean? She's got to be in heat."

*Like Spot*, I thought.

"Oh, just one more thing; I don't want to see any shit stains on her panties. 'Cause if I see shit stains on her panties, well then I'll just want to go home. I can't stand a woman who got shit stains on her panties."

And the speaker nodded. Winked at me. And entered the tent.

"How did I do?" Jim inquired.

I was impressed, I told him.

"Now what's going to happen?" he wondered.

"Well, he's either going to call you into the tent, or she's going to come out here. We just got to be patient."

The night had now wore on. And the Babel of voices up and down the midway appeared to have intensified. There were diatribes and exhortations, expositions and petty harangues, reasoned argument and dissertations. And then a few like at our present stop—one or two men making arrangements. Of mysterious sorts.

The flap of the tent opened. And she emerged. Jim's order. Blond hair with hundreds of tiny curls falling down onto the collar of the man's chesterfield coat he had given her to cover her naked body. Deep green eyes with eyelashes thick black and as long as miniature fans. They batted, kept fluttering anxiously. Expectantly. A deep moat of ruby red indelibly inscribed about her mouth which she formed into an O, approximately 2 millimeters in circumference. *Pi r squared*. And under the chesterfield coat one was not permitted to see the razor sharp tits that seemed to violently object their imprisonment by this coat. Like howitzer shells, the kind embedded in cement down at our World War II Honor Roll, they pointed unerringly toward Jim. And underneath, still cloaked by the chesterfield, was the belly he ordered. We could see it roll at command under the coat, like some soft but yet nameless creature of woman-sex in a dark room under the dark and warm covers. Yes. We were both excited now. All that we could ever imagine. *How had he done it, I mean my brother*, I thought? And she reached down smiling provocatively and gently took Jim's hand. And proceeded to lead it up the inside of her left leg, far up into the dark reaches under the chesterfield. Surely to assure him that once they were both naked, the Shirley Temple curls would be there.

And as the motion of their arms stopped, I watched Jim's face for a sign. And it came. Almost a beatific smile. And he looked at me and winked. Yep, it was Shirley Temple alright.

*The hole*, I thought. The hole. Check it out first. But his hand came out. He was satisfied.

"What about her tits?" I inquired.

But he admonished me. "What the hell is wrong with you, you asshole. Are you blind? Look at those bullets."

*Well, maybe it wasn't so funny after all*, I thought. He, Jim, had a determined look on his face now. There was no turning back. She and him were going to go inside that tent. And I would have to wait.

*Why in the hell couldn't I have taken it more seriously*, I thought. That little prick was going to go in there and come out happy. And as usual I'd wait outside.

So I was beginning to hate myself. And she reached down and took little Jim by the hand and began walking him toward the tent. But why was she wearing men's shoes, I wondered, black patent leather shoes.

IV

A short while later we were alone together on the midway, sort of between tents. I didn't want to show my ignorance by inquiring immediately of his time inside the tent. When he came out, we just sort of both walked casually away. He didn't seem any different than when he went in. I thought he would exit wearing a beard and smoking a pipe or something like that. No. He was, or appeared to be, the same old "Popeye's Dead" kid. After a few steps, he did stop and say he was hungry and asked if I would find him something to eat.

"Sure, in a minute," I replied.

"But how was it?" I really wanted to know.

"She really wanted me, Tom. I ain't ever seen anything hotter. Why, Jesus, she was just kissing and pawing all over me in the dark in there."

"She took off that coat, did she?"

"Why do you ask such a stupid question?" he scolded. "What do you think—I'm going to fuck her through the chesterfield?"

I hadn't known he knew the coat. But one hung in the old man's closet, and he wore it out only on special times. He must of had his eye on it, too. Little bastard.

"No, she just kissed me all over and I told her to wait. We'd get it all done. I wasn't going anywhere."

"Was there light in there, Jim? Could you really see?"

He couldn't believe I was so fucking stupid. "What do you have to see when you are putting your hand inside a woman's pussy?"

His hand! I was flabbergasted.

"The belly, the tits, the Shirley Temple curls, and the fire inside the hole . . . all those things?"

"Yep. Every one of them." And he said, "Look." He had made sure that nobody was looking, unbuttoned the fly of his pants and pulled out a limp peter. The goddamned thing was all purple and red. Like it had been held too close to a blow dryer. He proudly put it back into his pants. "That sonofabitch ain't going to want to go stepping out again for some time." He laughed. And spat hard on the ground like I've seen the old man do.

He walked on ahead of me looking for something to eat. *You better believe it*, I thought.

And Popeye rolled over in his grave. Ashamed.

V

He looked a little tired now, tired and hungry. And he kind of brushed against me like when we were real kids, I leading him around through the stores, he wanting to go home.

"Hang on, Jim," I said. And began feeling a bit protective of him, sort of like the *Boys Town* picture. You know which one. I'd have to find him something to eat.

"Don't ever tell the old man I let you go into such a place," I warned him. He shook his head. No, it was clear he would never want to. Suddenly he seemed to have run down. Had begun to shiver a bit. "What the hell is wrong with you?" I asked. "It ain't cold here." But he wasn't talking now, just shivering. Shivering. "Do you want to go home?"

He wanted something to eat. He wanted to sit down somewhere with something to eat. Goddamnit anyway! I should have known better. Some goddamn scam back there. And how his prick was going to swell up like a fucking balloon, and the whole neighborhood would know, including the old man.

"Does it hurt?" I asked.

"No. It doesn't hurt." But then he opened his fly again and looked at it.

It looked like some rabid dog had bitten it.

Then he started to cry.

Christ, I felt bad. And he began spitting into his open fly.

"What the hell is wrong with you? Why are you doing that?"

It hurt. He said. Hurt bad. He thought he was going to vomit. And the spit made it hurt less. Did I have a handkerchief?

Yeah. And he took it in his hands, an end in each hand, twirled it a few times, then placed it, gently tied it about his prick. Spitting on it and the prick a few times before he did. The thing looked ugly now. He unsteadily buttoned up his pants. And said we better forget the food. Just take him home.

"I can't take you home like this. You just sit there. I'll go beg some food. The swelling will go down. It will go down. You dumb little shit."

And he cried and cried.

The cacophony of voices outside the many tents now seemed muted. People, the men, seemed to have wandered away. There were only a few stragglers left on the midway. Many of the speakers' boxes in front of the tent had been abandoned. A few weren't, but no one seemed too interested anymore.

I had wanted to do so many things this night. So many tents I wanted to enter. The list of speakers I wanted to hear seemed endless. But it was all so barren now. Like some mysterious force had cracked the spine of this place, beat the life out of it. The tongue of Babel—it was as if my brother had mysteriously swallowed it in seizure.

The midway had a dank and vacant feeling to it now. And the speakers—those professors of homiletics, of science, of philosophy, of literature and the few shamans among them—why those that I saw who remained looked like copies, cheap copies of the man in the chesterfield coat, with his mustache and his black patent leather shoes. The night was going to be so wonderfully long, I thought wistfully.

Why, it had only begun. I had just started to get an idea of these treasure-filled tents and their ferry men for the river Acheron. Perhaps, I had thought earlier, I would be able to take home a new voice—'*Baruch Atah Elohim*'; or at least leave speaking more knowledgeably about life.

I had heard one of the speakers exclaim, "An unexamined life is not worth living." That, too, had aroused my curiosity.

But the speakers were mostly gone now. The few that were left were creeps. And Jim, Popeye Jim, clearly wanted to go home.

Christ, I wondered, I still got to go over that fucking bridge tomorrow and I ain't learned one goddamned thing here tonight that's going to help me in any way.

And with Jim beside me, walking like he had been kicked in the balls, and me worrying about killing myself—*well life ain't all that fun*, I thought.

And the two of us cried like babies driving back to the house in the old man's car.

# PASSING THROUGH AMBRIDGE

*T*HEY GAVE ME a track lantern, but I had to buy the mattress-ticking cap. I asked Katy to pick me up a metal dinner bucket. "One of those that look like a silver-dome mobile home." The railroaders all carried them.

I'd been anxious to get into the man's game for some time. When I stepped off the bus in Mahoningtown at dusk, about a mile's walk from the Baltimore & Ohio roundhouse, a kerchief knotted about my neck and sporting a new pair of steel-toed clodhoppers, it smelled and felt like the real thing. The couple nights a week at the archaic weight room in the local YMCA had begun to pay off, too.

Railroad tracks—one sure way out of town—held a special romance for me. The tracks were the primary source of the strange men who camped out at the brickyards near our house, nesting down alongside the ovens during the cold months. A week wouldn't pass that one of these "vagrants" didn't show up at our backdoor begging for food or coins in exchange for some odd job. Unkempt and smelling bad, they'd settle for a bologna sandwich and an orange in a paper sack that Katy would dangle outside the screen door like it was a dead mouse.

The tracks carried the circus and carnival into town, too. And once near Christmas, our old man took my brother, Westley, and me to Radio City Music Hall by rail. The first time the three of us had ever been out of Hebron. When we passed through the outskirts of Ambridge, Pap told us that all the bridges in America were built there. From the railcar we could see story-high AMBRIDGE letters on a factory building.

"Even the Golden Gate Bridge?" I asked.

"All of them, Son," he said.

"The Brooklyn Bridge, too?" Westley asked.

"That, too," Pap replied.

I had a difficult time imagining this small Pennsylvania town fabricating those mighty dream bridges over a piddley-ass river that ran in front of the plant. But when we got to New York City and I saw all those tall skyscrapers stacked up next to each other, their marble and gold lobbies tall as Hebron's Masonic Temple, I was ready to believe anything.

Pap was the eye-opener of our family. Been up to our mother, Westley and me would've kept our eyes shut. Even later on in her life, Katy'd said, "I've seen enough." But Pap, when he died, I specifically ordered Mr. Nolde, the mortician, to leave Pap's eyes open. When we found him lying cold on the kitchen floor one morning, they were wide awake. Maybe he'd pass through Ambridge, I thought.

Dexter Connaughton, my track boss, handed me a janitor's broom and pointed me to the supply depot just outside the roundhouse. My shift ran from 8 p.m. to 4 a.m. Weren't quite an hour passed before Cannaughton showed up to check on me. Katy had taught me good work habits. She'd walked every lawn I'd ever mowed. If it wasn't done to her satisfaction, she'd drag me back, apologize to the Mrs., and then the two of us would mow and trim until it suited her. But Connaughton wore a look of disapproval across his pudding face.

"What is it, sir?" I said.

"You aimin' to keep this job for the whole summer, boy?"

"Yessir," I said. "I like it here, sir." They paid good union wages.

"Then you'd better brighten up—fast."

He was eluding me.

"You watch anybody else work around here?"

"My second day, sir. Ain't had much chance to observe."

"How long you think this here job should take, Daugherty?"

"I guess I should have been done by now, huh?"

"Done?" he laughed, surveying the storage depot floor. "One week, Daugherty. This job should take you at least one damn week."

"One week! I'll be done in a half hour, sir."

"Then pick up your paycheck. And don't bother coming back tomorrow, 'cause there won't be a goddamn thing for you to do."

Katy would have shit. This was contrary to everything I knew about giving an honest day's work in return for an honest dollar. Connaughton standing there ordering me to loaf, but pretend I was working. I wasn't hired to work on the railroad; I was hired for summer stock, evening shift. And after I began observing my fellow workers, damn if they weren't all actors, too. A crew would spend all night hauling supplies from the storage depot to the roundhouse. The next evening they'd trestle them back to the supply depot again. All these grown men working the night railyards, lanterns swinging from their sides, moving around like fireflies. Not one damn honest night's labor occurring.

The fifth day of my employment, Connaughton directed me to an unhitched caboose out in the railyard, saying I'd find my crew inside. "Report to the caboose for the remainder of the summer, Daugherty," he wheezed. Smoke rose out of its stovepipe chimney and as I got closer, I could hear chortling inside.

"C&O, go see who's at our door," a gruff voice ordered.

C&O, short for Chesapeake & Ohio, welcomed me in. Four bandanna-necked men sat around a potbelly stove drinking out of their tin lunch pail cups and playing poker on the caboose lunch table. Each was comfortably seated on upholstered railcar seat cushions with illuminated red caution bulbs on their rail lanterns alongside, creating a seasonal atmosphere. It was damn hot in the caboose. All of the men except C&O had stripped down to their undershirts. The temperature outside wasn't below 70°. One man—I presume the crew foreman—motioned me to sit down alongside C&O, who was sitting out the game. Along the inside walls of the caboose were seat rails appointed by these mohair seat cushions.

"Why's it so damn hot?" I asked C&O, staring at the cheesecake calendars tacked above the players' heads.

"Sal likes it that way."

"Why? It's summer outside."

"Sal says he got to work up a sweat somehow."

I started to laugh. C&O didn't.

It must have been 90° in the caboose. I stripped down, but didn't have any undershirt on. Finally the game was over. Sal rose.

"What's your name?"

"Daugherty. Jimmy Daugherty."

"Your old man a railroader?"

"No, sir."

"How'd the fuck you get in here?"

"State Unemployment Office."

"You're a liar, Daugherty."

"Honest to God," I said. The three at the poker table looked like they were about to jump me. C&O held his head down. I knew about rites of initiation.

"You got to know somebody to work on the fucking Baltimore and Ohio railroad, Daugherty. Who in the hell is it? Don't give us any shit, boy." Sal wasn't letting up.

"Maybe it's his mother," a heavyset, mustachioed worker drawled.

They all laughed. C&O tried to suppress his, clearly embarrassed by this confrontation.

"Your mother a gandy dancer?" another heckled. "You know Daugherty's mother, C&O?"

C&O began to blush. Then giggle. Like somebody was fingering him under his armpits, jukin' his ribs. He began to writhe in laughter, and his skeletal frame fell to the caboose floor, spittle seeping out the sides of his mouth. At first the men watched him bemusedly, then they, too, began to laugh. Soon, all of the men were laughing uproariously and emitting loud gas noises. I stood shirtless in the corner of the caboose, humorless. When the spell petered out, Sal addressed me.

"Well?"

"I'm here for the summer. Connaughton said you were short a man."

"*Short a man!*" Sal croaked. He ran out of the caboose and pissed up against its side, caught in the paroxysm of laughter that once again had gripped the crew.

A factory whistle shattered the gaiety.

"Chow time!" C&O yelled.

We gathered around the caboose card table and opened our metal buckets.

"Welcome, Daugherty," Sal said. "We don't like pricks working with us. But a schoolboy needs help. When the summer job is over, put a fucking lid on it, boy. Don't ever come back. Look at us."

They did look like a sorry bunch. Sal was the only one who looked intelligent. He had the upper body of a boxer. And straight black hair Brilliantined to his head. Clean-shaven, with a Clorox-white undershirt. He wore a spotless pair of khaki pants that he or his wife had sewn a crease in. The other men, excluding C&O, were nondescript types. Reuben affected a mustache and a two-day-old beard, always. He also wore a navy pea coat even in the hottest weather. Except in the hot caboose, when it hung on a hook behind him. Reuben was grossly overweight—his undershirts all had a yellowish cast with a hole at the midriff, and an industrial-weight belt cinched so severely he looked like a knockwurst.

Otto and Sydney were older, bespectacled types. Like two vagrants who spent their time in libraries reading week-old newspapers. Each was always arguing with the other about politics. I sensed they were some kind of washed-up Party sympathizers. Sal would get impatient with their wrangling and tell them Stalin was a Sicilian who was jerkin' them both off. But Otto and Sydney dismissed Sal, since they were intellectuals and he wasn't. Each huddled about him like he were the caboose stove, however, even in the middle of July.

And C&O was a simpleton.

He couldn't read, spell, or count and was dropped off to work each evening, then met at the guard's gate at 4 a.m. by his emaciated mother, Rose Calucca. Carrying or sweeping he could do, tasks that had to be closely monitored by Sal—who was paternal toward him (sometimes sadistic). Both had Italian ancestry, and lived a few short streets from each other in Mahoningtown, close to the roundhouse. C&O's brother, Junior Calucca, was a Baltimore & Ohio switch foreman on day shift—had been for nearly two decades—and when mother Rose Calucca grew too old and feeble to handle C&O, Junior finagled him a permanent job on the evening shift with Sal's supply crew. (Sal was getting some vigorish on the side, we suspected.)

If you asked C&O to carry a carton of wiping rags, say, a hundred yards to the pumping station, after fifty he'd forget where he was going and return to the beginning, asking for fresh directions. He was perfect for the railroad play-acting job. My first night with the crew, watching the four play cards until 1 a.m., I was startled to hear Sal announce it was time to work. The fire had died out. We dressed to go outside the caboose, where Sal directed us to hand-truck thirty five-gallon cans of lubrication to the roundhouse for the steam engines. The following evening we carted them all back to the supply depot, short six—what the roundhouse requisitioned in the first place.

In the second week of my employment, I had the routine down. We'd meet in the caboose, I'd ignite a small fire in the potbelly stove, pour booze Sal had purloined from the B&O boardroom into each thermos, lay the cards out—and a game would ensue. I didn't play, choosing instead to read books in the caboose's corner.

"Do what you want, Daugherty," the men obliged.

Occasionally one of them would ask what I was reading. Sydney would pull some political material he wanted me to read out of his lunch bucket. But it never went much further than that—my education on class warfare. I didn't ask enough questions for Sydney, and after a time, he wrote me off. Hart Crane and Nathaniel West held my interest.

C&O, cradling a small battery-operated portable radio, would often sit next to me listening to any music he could find on the bands. When he played it too loud, Sal would bark at him. Like a chastised dog, C&O'd bow his head down to his knees, then after several moments, draw the radio up close to his ear. He and I seldom exchanged words. Curious to see what I had in my lunch each day, he'd set his bucket next to mine on the cushions. (I think the whole south side of Hebron had several of these cushions in their houses; Sal kept requisitioning more from the central depot in Akron.)

\* \* \*

One night, Salvatore greeted us in the caboose wearing a suit jacket and tie. He stood solemnly in front of the cold stove.

"Boys, tonight I got something special to announce."

C&O, normally the most curious, bowed his head and began to tremble.

"Do you tell them, C&O—or do I?"

C&O shook his head determinedly.

"OK," Sal said. "C&O's getting married in two weeks."

It had to be one of DiCenza's demonic jokes.

Sydney stared angrily at Sal, like he'd gone too far in taking advantage of C&O's simple wit.

"C&O's wife-to-be arrives in Mahoningtown two weeks from Friday. The wedding ceremony will take place at St. Vitus's Church that Saturday morning. Sunday, C&O and . . ." Sal paused, then looked over at C&O, who by now had cradled his head in his hands and shook in a kind of rapturous trance, half laughing, half crying. Sal cracked him alert with a command:

"C&O, tell them her name!"

C&O stood at attention. "Bernadette," he replied.

"*Bernadette!*" we shouted.

C&O shook his head, echoing our disbelief. Then started to chortle again; the saliva began to gather at the corners of his spectral mouth. Spasms. Sal grabbed him, again chastising him: "Get a hold of yourself! Do you think she wants to crawl in bed with some blathering idiot?"

We couldn't suppress our laughter. C&O couldn't either. He was the butt of our outrageous humor. He felt he *belonged* when we laughed at him. Gestures he thought obscene, he'd nervously flash. Popping his cheek with his index finger made us roar the hardest. But Sal chastised us for pushing C&O over the line. "This is serious shit," he reprimanded. "The poor fuck is getting married, and we got to help him pull it off."

Every one of us drew inward. Even C&O, as if he were trying to fathom the mysteries that lay ahead. *C&O with a wife? A house? Pens of chickens and rabbits? Children?* It was a miracle, a testament to families helping families and the corrupt B&O management and its union that C&O was even on a payroll. The Catholic Church couldn't have accomplished such goodness.

"Sal, where is this saint coming from?" Reuben asked, looking around at us.

"Italy," came Sal's terse response.

"She ever see C&O?"

"Nope."

"He see her?" Sydney was incredulous.

"Pictures her mother sent Rose Calucca. Bernadette's mother and Rose went to school together in Calabria," Sal said.

"What's she gonna say when she gets off the boat and sees C&O?" I asked.

"She's gonna take the train to Mahoningtown," Sal said. "We're all gonna meet the train. Mrs. Calucca, brother Junior, me and C&O. Ain't nobody gonna say a damn word. Bernadette's gonna step off the train, I'm gonna step forward, kiss her on the cheek, and walk her back to the family leaning up against the station house. We're all gonna get in the undertaker's car and go to the Sons of Italy club and have a big meal, drinking and dancing and speeches—stuff like that. Me, Bernadette, Rose Calucca, Junior and C&O all at the head table. Be like that all night! Bernadette dances with Junior, dances with me, and maybe even dances with C&O."

"You going to snooker her, Sal? On the poor woman's wedding night, you gonna snooker her?" Reuben asked.

"Should I let her see the goat before dinner?" Sal shot back. "The whole goddamn thing stinks. But what are you gonna do? His old lady wants it before she dies. She wants C&O to be off with a family like me and Junior. You, Reuben. Sydney, Otto, the rest of us—even boy-Daugherty. *Don't C&O deserve it?*"

Sal was getting lathered up.

"Ain't Bernadette's fault either, is it, Sal?" Sydney said.

"Hey, she wants to come to America, don't she?"

"When you gonna let her know C&O's the one?" Otto asked.

"Bedtime."

"*Bedtime?*" we chorused.

"She's been quaffing the bubbly and dancing, huh? Too shy to ask is it Junior or me. '*Who's the one?*' Before midnight, we push C&O up the steps to the nuptial bedroom they got over the Sons of Italy dining hall. The goat's lying up there stretched out between starched sheets waiting for the fair Bernadette ... and she's a beauty, man. Show 'em the pictures, C&O."

C&O, who had been listening raptly, not understanding a word, pulled the photographs out of his shirt pocket. Tobacco juice stains mar Bernadette's face, and the shots are dog-eared like old playing cards. But the bride-to-be was just how Sal described her. A real tomato. They had her attired in a black mourning dress with a white doily covering her head. But she was wearing this demure "Going-to-America" smile.

"Looks gullible," sniffed Sydney.

"At midnight Junior or me coaxes her up the nuptial stairs, we open the goat's door, shove her in, and padlock it. *She knows what she got to do.* Mrs. Calucca and her church cronies be waiting sentinel downstairs, drinking black coffee until morning to ascertain the consummation transpired.

"*No blood, no America.* Only shame. Bernadette's shipped back home Sunday night."

At first, we were confused. Not only was Bernadette marrying an imbecile, but she had to be a *virgin, too*? When I looked at Sal for some kind of explanation, he just shrugged, and sat down with the other crew members at the card table. He pulled his shirt and tie off and dealt the cards.

\* \* \*

C&O developed a nervous twitch near his wedding day. Sal periodically gave him a whack on his back, trying to break the habit. Sal claimed it was stress. That, like a goat being led out of his pen at night alone, C&O knew he was going to get garroted. Sal had butchered enough pigs and sheep in his sheds in Mahoningtown, so he spoke with authority.

"Those poor bastards always know when they are about to be slaughtered."

"What's Bernadette going to do when she sees C&O lying like a fruitcake in her wedding bed?" Otto asked.

Sal thought for a moment.

"Take pity on the poor cocksucker? How do I know?

"You think she wants to go back to Calabria, stain her feet in the grape juice? So she bleeds a few drops for the goat. Christ, she's slept in the manger! She's a Calabrian. Those dames ain't no Neapolitans, are they Reuben?"

Reuben agreed.

"You melancholic bastards. Just hope she's a virgin. Rose Calucca and her harpies will take their fists to her if she ain't. Her bringing disgrace to C&O, Father Vignale and the entire St. Vitus parish. Those old ladies all want their daughters to marry a fool. The Christ child. No malingerers and philanderers like most of us here. Us good-for-nothings. C&O's a good-for-something. *You got it?* He's the innocent. The bitch just better play it right."

"Do you think Bernadette's old lady is in on the scam?" I asked.

"America's the scam! So what if he can't read or write? He got a job, huh?" C&O smiled proudly. "Maybe he gives her a bambino. What more could she ask?"

\* \* \*

First, my home education about the morality of working, putting in an honest day's labor for an honest dollar in return, had shit the bed. Now the institution of marriage was being fiddled with big time. And two days before C&O's big wedding, he took off sick. Sal said it was the hives, then became uptight about the subject, refusing to discuss it. The wedding day came and passed without any of us—except Sal of course—being invited. The next week he didn't mention it. When Reuben boldly broached the subject, Sal went outside in a snit and pissed up against our red caboose.

It weren't until one week after the "honeymoon" C&O appeared. Christ, he looked different. He weren't so silly anymore. "Of more serious mien" is how I'd describe him. He weren't so quick to snicker anymore either. Kind of like the rest of the men. Except now instead of sitting alone while they played cards and listening to music, he read religious tracts.

Well, "read" is too strong of a term.

Each day in his dinner bucket he brought new booklets he'd picked up in the anteroom of St. Vitus, tracts on marriage and the like. I asked him the second day if he wanted me to read them aloud. Shyly, he said yes. So while Sal and the crew played twenty-one, I read these homilies on marriage, fealty, and parenting to C&O. He sat next to me piously in the caboose like a novice monk. I felt like Thomas Merton.

\* \* \*

Sal permitted none of us in his presence to question C&O about the wedding night or its aftermath. C&O's brother, Junior, told somebody in the switch house that Rose and her neighbors did awaken the betrothed that Sunday morning before dawn to impatiently examine the wedding sheets for blood; then crowed when they spotted it, pushing the betrothed aside as they ran back down the nuptial steps into the streets singing.

But it wasn't until about a month later, a Saturday morning just before winding up the work week, that Sal, after a full evening of cards and drinking, turned and asked C&O how he liked *poontang*.

The old paroxysms ensued.

"Tell us, C&O, is it nice and juicy like Otto said it would be?"

C&O nodded vigorously.

"You see her naked yet?" Sal asked. Reuben surveyed the leg art.

What the hell was this about, I wondered.

"Tell us, C&O, you see her naked? And has she got *big* ones, C&O?"

C&O knew what Sal was asking. He ceased snickering. Like he was embarrassed. Sal had overstepped his bounds. C&O never acted like this before. But DiCenza kept pressing.

"C&O, what's her pussy look like in the daylight?"

Pulling his engineer's hat down over his ears, C&O stood up, spat in his right hand and flung it straight at Sal's face. Then stomped out of the caboose. The room remained quiet for a full minute. Sal was chagrined. We'd never seen C&O take offense at his friend and "brother."

"He's seen her naked, ain't he?" Sal asked accusingly. "The sonofabitch. She's stood before him in the morning light, ain't she? Well, speak up you assholes!"

Otto shuffled the deck with one hand, nervously eyeing Sydney.

"She's stood before the idiot without a stitch of clothes on, ain't she? Naked as the Mediterranean by the bedside lamp. Her raven hair running down to the pit of her ass and those god-almighty, sun-blessed, peach tits he's eyeballed. And the dimple in her belly, the grove of navel hairs—the vineyard, the berry farm, the black forest, the labial grave. The tongue cozy. Sonofabitch. Old C&O's seen it all! Ain't he?"

Sal, in a jealous rage, tossed the card table against the wall, and jumped up. The caboose shook. We clustered over by the benches. Sal kicked the stove and smacked against it with his bare hands like a wounded animal.

"What the fuck's wrong with you, Sal?" Reuben cried.

Sal gathered himself, poured some liquor from the thermos into his cup.

"Twenty years. Count them." His angry hands, he opened and clenched them mechanically. "Twenty. And not once, even in the moonlight—for the shades are always drawn—have I ever got to see my *Donna* naked. Even in the measly crack under our doorway when the hall light is creeping in, she covers it up with a towel. Our bedroom—black as the woods.

"Not once has Salvatore got to see how her tits hang off her mighty chest. How her ass curves in the morning light. What the tongue cozy looks like in the sun. *All in my imagination. My hands see, my fucking thighs see, my dick sees . . . BUT SAL DON'T SEE!*"

He jabbed at these parts of his anatomy.

"With this finger I could fucking draw her navel on paper for each of you, but I ain't ever seen it with *these*!" He jabbed his eyes. "Or the crack of her ass. Or the *CRYING VIRGIN*.

*"Where's the Justice, I ask?"*

Sydney vainly gestured to Sal to take a seat.

"Bernadette gets off the Queen Mary and unveils, huh? Snow slides off her temple. The gown slides off her coppery bosom straight into the New York Harbor, and our fool drops to his knees, trembling. All the cocksuckers in Battery Park run to rattle their windows. The Staten Island Ferries steam-whistle. And the fucking Stature of Liberty shimmers naked?

"Right in Manhattan harbor, for Chrissake! Rose and her widowed crows run through Battery Park shouting—*Blood on the sheets! There's blood on the sheets!*—bed linens flagging their clothesline poles. And Gotham's fire boats spray jets of water up against Liberty's bare ass? Good Lady Liberty's getting the old morning-after douche?

"But where's the fucking justice, I ask? Answer me, Sydney!"

Sal leapt up on the bench, punting C&O's lunch bucket against the caboose door.

"And Donna DiCenza's still keeping *ME—Her Sal*—in the dark? *What am I? A fucking dago married to Helen Keller? What is it with the goose worship in this land?*

"Why do they always get the breaks?"

The four of us, chastened, sat hunched over the card table. Several minutes passed before Sal quietly pulled up a chair.

"Sydney, go outside and let C&O in," he said.

"But I don't know where he went, Sal. Christ, he could be anywhere out there in the dark."

"He ain't," Sal said, shuffling the deck like a Nevada croupier. "He's pissing up against the caboose."

I looked out the window. In the blackness, white steam rose off a *Silver Phantom* that shot triumphantly out of Chesapeake & Ohio—his parabolic dream—arcing the rails, to hit then splash-die against our deserted car.

*We are passing through Ambridge*, I thought.

# BANJO GREASE

"**S**KYLINE DRIVE-IN? YOU mean on the outskirts of Niles?"

"I think so."

"It sure as hell's closed, boy."

"I know that. My uncle works there."

"He'll be waiting for you at 2 a.m.?"

"Yeah."

"You ain't ever been there?"

"No, Sir."

A passenger seated directly behind the Greyhound driver spoke up. "Bill, that place shuts down at midnight."

"His uncle's meeting him there. Ain't that what you said, son?"

Flat terrain poked by scrub pine lay in a fluorescent haze before him. No houses, barns, or industrial buildings. A sharp odor of sulfuric acid penetrated the night air. He'd noticed the many automobile salvage establishments lining the roadway entering Niles interspersed by trailer parks. The lone church he saw—outlined like a license plate in heliotrope neon—three metal trailers joined to form a cross.

He began walking. In short distances he'd spot blighted car seats, a drive shaft, lead batteries tossed into the weeds. A Pontiac grill capped a pyramid of tires man-high. Oil cans catching rain and breeding mosquitoes lay nearby. And in the far distance, an orange-rust nimbus rose liquidly on the horizon. Strings of incandescent bulbs, line after shimmering line—hundreds of them—

loped effortlessly into the black sky, festooning a copper refinery like a shoaled freighter.

But most everything clung low to the ground here in Niles—including its trees. The workers now home in their trailer beds, they, too, thought Westley, lie close to the soil to escape this blanket of methane stench. The whole burg could pick up and vanish overnight, a herd of tin elephants stopping for an occasional shit in its streams. Along their roadsides.

Westley stepped out of the glare of the oncoming headlights into the scrub. Next to him lay a pair of muslin dolls about whose bisque heads coiled a vermillion jumping rope, and above, dangling from a brush-alder, a cellulose monkey, phlegm spitting out its runty eyes. The automobile slowed then stopped. Its rear door sprang open and out jumped a young man, naked waist down, laughing riotously with the nude he pulled out after him. In white plastic boots she took flight into the field, tripping over debris, then crouching behind a metal drum. Both laughing so hard now, neither barely stood upright as he drew her back to the Chevrolet, draping her against its trunk.

A Campbell's cream of asparagus soup container, its distinctive red-and-white label still intact—the shaved-head reveler slid over his erect member then proceeded to dance a two-step towards her. Unamused, she waved him off. He gazed about him once more and spied a walker clumped together with a porcelain bedpan; clutching the walker and feigning an exaggerated infirmity of stride, he resumed his approach—the Campbell's soup can still firmly sheathing his cock. She smiled, but no surrender.

"Get the fuck on her, will you, Pete? For Christ's sake!" the men cried impatiently from the car.

Displaying a heightened sense of urgency, he grabbed a dinette chair missing its seat, gingerly retrieved the bedpan, looked distractedly about him until he spotted a velvet chapeau . . . but still unsatisfied, skirmished about in a pile of face creams and bathroom sundries . . . then abruptly, with theatrical flourish, placed the damaged chair before him, welcomed himself to sit, situated the bedpan under its hole, and collapsed. His ass fell several inches beneath the seat's rim. Unruffled, he crossed his legs lady-like, the Campbell's soup can now rising to a near vertical, brandished the sodden chapeau over his shaved pate, and archly observed:

"The service around here is lousy."

The young woman began to giggle, sashayed over to him, and drew the soup can off his still-erect member. He didn't remove his hat while she ate him.

At the intersection of DeForest Road and Trumbull County Highway, Westley turned eastward, approaching a commercial bakery. Its trucks he'd seen back in Hebron: a child with Shirley Temple curls biting into a slice of white bread slathered heavily with sunny butter adorning their bright red sides. The strong odor of the baking bread masked the odor of sulfuric acid to which he was slowly becoming acclimated. He felt pangs of hunger. And wondered once again if he was doing the right thing. A used trailer lot sat alongside the bakery. He'd never seen one of these. Used car lots abounded in Hebron. But a used home lot—on Firestones and Goodyears? *Maybe that's what the hell's gone wrong in Hebron? People froze right up back there. Like a bad transmission. Here the church has wheels.*

Suddenly, arcing the night sky in giant red neon and yellow script and making loud electrical noises, the massive windowless facade of *SKYLINE DRIVE-IN THEATRE* loomed—*TRUMBULL COUNTY'S FINEST.* A glass ticket booth outlined in purple neon tubes sat jewel-like and beckoning in the center of its gravel entrance. Pin spotlights shone down onto a chromium and leather chair inside, microphones suspended from the booth's ceiling as if it were the cockpit of a giant airship. But the rest of the outdoor theater stood in ghostly darkness.

Except in the far back row. Forlorn, abutting the scrub brush meadow, sat an aluminum trailer. A modest affair on wheels, enclosed by a white picket-fence skirt, its skin rounded, riveted zephyr-like, glinting in the argent moonlight like a farm pond. Westley quickly recognized George and Min's 1942 forest-green Plymouth coupe parked at its rear.

Westley hammered loudly on the metal trailer's door:

"*Hello, Aunt Min. Hello, Uncle George. It's me—Westley. Westley Daugherty.*"

There was no sound.

He beat harder. Suddenly a light came on near the front end of the mobile home. The vehicle tremorred slightly. It rocked as would a boat in its slip. Someone is walking down a very small hallway, he thought. Christ, it looks like a submarine.

"*It's Westley, from Hebron! Hello! Westley, ME!*"

Westley waved his arms to put on notice anybody who might be looking out that it was indeed him. And not a thief. He didn't want near-deaf George to drop him with his pistol. George couldn't see all that well either. The last visit he had taken a right up the goddamn Baltimore and Ohio tracks over near Mahoningtown, and bounced the Plymouth over several dozen cross ties before acknowledging he'd made a wrong turn.

"*Hey, Uncle George, it's me. WESTLEY! I'M ALL ALONE!*"

The small metal door opened a crack and Westley heard Min's voice.

"Who in the hell is here?"

"It's me! Westley. Your boy . . . remember?"

Like the lid of a can, the trailer door slowly opened. A sweet and stale odor rose out of its aperture. Min suddenly appeared, her henna shoe-polished hair curled in scraps of toilet paper with metal rollers the size of silver-dollar wrappers. Her rouged cheeks, splotched and smeared, sinking in towards her mouth—upper and lower dentures back in a jar at bedside, soaking. A floral house dress zippered frontally draped her massive frame and lard-sack breasts hung pendulously down onto her globe of a stomach—mounds of flesh cascading upon mounds of flesh, all of it indecorously veiled by a great expanse of jonquil-patterned percale stopping just short of her feet: misshapen and covered with corns and bunions like barnacles, and resting flat as pancakes on the trailer's linoleum floor.

"There just ain't any room for you, Westley! Whatever got it in your mind to come here in the first place?"

*Your warm flesh. The mounds and mounds of it, Min. I wanted to be smothered by warmth and fed your pancakes—high stacks of them—until I succumbed and woke up a fucking man like George, perhaps.*

"You told me I was always welcome, Aunt Min. You always said, 'If they don't want you, you get right away to Aunt Min's. Everybody loves Aunt Min. I'll see that you are taken care of.'" A kind of mantra I unleashed at her with a slight degree of hurt and confusion mixed in. I held my head down, staring at her feet.

"GEORGE!" she screamed.

It startled me. I stepped away from the tiny ship on wheels.

"GEORGE! Margaret's boy Westley's here!"

Min stepped out onto the grass like some wraith who'd escaped off one of the drive-in's picture shows. Back in Hebron she looked pleasantly old, always nicely attired in a dress, the sort worn by older women to church on Sunday; her face all powdered and rouged up, and her hair, a kind of orange-brown, wrapped tightly about her large head. Her low-heeled shoes had, however, looked painfully uncomfortable as her wide feet spilled out over their weakened sides. (I thought they looked like eggplants stuffed with feet.)

But now, staring at me in her shoe-polished hair, clearly applied with the cloth dauber right out of a bottle of Shinola liquid several strands at a time to its dwindling mass, you could see splotches on her forehead and ears where the dauber missed. And the metal rollers catching the glint of the moonlight just like her trailer top. Her mouth—all misshapen and contorted, no teeth to assist in a more diplomatic composure—sucking in and out with quick and heavy breaths like a dream fish I'd ruefully hooked at the rear of Trumbull County's finest, *Skyline Drive-in*. Min was apoplectic. Her lips pursed and angry as the ass of a simian monkey; long gray hairs rose forlornly out of her chin; a lump of flesh the size of a fist beat heart-like at her larynx. And the great breasts rolled back and forth across the top of her stomach like ball sacks while she stood waving her arms, first towards her and George's little metal home—then back at me . . . Westley Daugherty, *night intruder.*

I had interrupted them at the high point of their cinematic life.

Mimicking small nocturnal animals, her feet slid back and forth on the Skyline's grass inside the cute little picket fence.

George finally appeared at the trailer's door. Min I took at her word. Believed until now everything she said. Also, mother never hugged me as warmly as Min always did. I liked being enveloped in all that hot and steamy, sweet-stale smelling woman's flesh. And she could make those delicious pancakes, stacks of them the size of drink coasters. Mother made them sparingly, the size of dinner plates. I relished eating Aunt Min's cakes: one could stack them up the height of a geometry book on end and pour maple syrup down over them like golden honey. You had to eat them early morning, too, so the sunlight rushing into the kitchen shone through the viscous liquid as it rained down over the stack's roof then slowly dripped down off its sides.

It weren't the same eating them after dark.

But George I liked without reserve, for he had this wordless habit of periodically grabbing my hand or arm and rolling his large thumb, index, and middle fingers back and forth across my bones—like he was kneading them. He'd scrunch up his mouth when he was doing this, but with a smile in his eyes. It was always very funny, I thought, but eventually I'd have to holler for him to let go because it soon began to hurt.

"Do you give up?"

Invariably I'd say I did.

"Good," he'd reply. And in mock reprimand, "Don't ever let me catch you doing it again." Just as quickly he'd return to his newspaper.

When George awoke in the morning at our house, I could hear him rolling on the floor of my mother and father's bedroom which they'd abandon. Once I gently opened their bedroom door a crack and peered in: George, in a yellowing pair of long johns, clear stains on the trap-door's ass, was somersaulting on the linoleum. Two one way, two back again. Again and again. Until he finally noticed me staring at him.

"What the hell do you want?" he demanded in that mock scolding voice.

And chased me down the stairs. But it was always a joke with him. He never said but a word or two at the dinner table ... and left the chatter to Min. He called her "Mommy."

*Mommy, do you want me to drive home?*

*Mommy, what time do you want to leave?*

After supper one evening, he told a story to my father, my brother, James, and me once the dishes had been cleared away. Mother and Min had retired to the living room.

"One night Mommy and me wanted to make some pouchy pie. 'George, go to the medicine cabinet and get the jar of Vaseline,' she said. Well, I didn't bother to turn the light on, and went in and fiddled around in the cabinet and found the jar and after I removed its lid, I slathered up real good and took it in and handed it to Mommy. And she did the same. Just as we begun doing it, Jesus Christ I felt like she had taken a blowtorch to my pecker: I *hooped* out of bed and ran out into the backyard fanning my cock like it were aflame. And *hooping* just as loud was Mommy, following me like she'd been set on fire, too.

"'God Almighty!' she cried. 'Get a bucket of water! For Chrissake, George, do something.' It was like her vagina was melting, you know. Here I was still jumpin' around on the ground waiting for my pecker to rocket off the hinge of my ass like a $10 firecracker and her screaming to me toss water on her Abraham Lincoln.

"The poor sonofabitch had caught on fire by smokin' in bed."

Along about now the three of us were lying across the table laughing hard.

George solemnly continued. "I grabbed my pecker with my hand, squeezin' it harder than I ever before dared to let it feel *real* pain, and ran inside and grabbed from the Frigidaire a quart of cold milk. Back out into the night I ran over to Mommy who was now lying on her back in the grass with her legs spread wider than I knew she could and crying ... just like she'd made love to the man in the moon ... and poured damn near the entire quart all over Abe Lincoln's jaw."

Then he just stared at us until we quieted down.

"What happened to Aunt Min?" James asked.

"Oh, she quieted down."

"What the hell was in the jar?" my father asked.

"*Banjo Grease,*" he replied.

Now standing in the doorway, "Westley!" he exclaimed. "What the hell did you do, son?" He stepped out of the trailer, grabbed my arm and slowly began kneading the bone between his muscular fingers like he always did. Slowly a smile rose to his face. When I was about ready to holler; he held up his other hand, stopping me.

"*Wait,*" he whispered. "*You'll wake the neighbors.* Tomorrow you and me will clean up the rubber jimmies and the panties they throw out the windows. Mommy don't like doing that. She just gags and spits when she has to do that. We'll look for money, too. Always some money lying about. Then when Mommy takes her long nap, we'll go fishing. You and me, catch a raft of sunfish over at Mosquito Lake if the sulphur from the refinery don't itch your throat too much.

"Whadaya say, son?"

"Fine."

Then finally he squeezed real hard. I made a sound.

"Do you give up?" he demanded.

I nodded that I did.

"Good, goddamnit. Don't ever do it again!"

He pushed me toward the opening of the metal container. "Mommy, get Westley a bed ready on our davenport."

\* \* \*

I stayed on a couple of days, but slept in their Plymouth coupe and rarely spent anytime at all inside the trailer. Min might invite me in for a sandwich. At night before the show I'd eat hamburgers at the concession stand or travel up the road a way and eat lunch at the local dairy. Periodically I'd knock on the trailer door to use the bathroom. Mostly I waited around for George. Once Min traveled over into the meadow behind the drive-in to pick blueberries for a pie she was going to make and asked George and me to join. We picked several quarts but the pie never got baked.

In the morning he'd start at one end of the first row of Skyline speakers, me at the other end and we'd both work our way toward its center. We carried big canvas bags like garbage men, wore gloves and picked up everything that was left behind. It was not uncommon to find half-eaten ribs of beef or pork chop bones. Potato skins, sardine cans, of course all brands of beer and whiskey bottles, and most of all, chicken bones. Just like George said, weren't a row that we'd clean up but that he or I didn't have to pick up several used condoms. And what set my imagination aflame was to come across a pair of ladies' undergarments.

He claimed you could always tell what kind of panties-day it was going to be depending on what the main feature was. Ray Milland, Jimmy Stewart, and Burt Lancaster, George swore, always produced the biggest number of tossed-out-the-window underwear. But there seemed to be no correlation between the number of condoms and panties. The former remaining constant. George thought the ratio between empty popcorn boxes and used rubbers was about 5 to 1. And I did find money, a $10 bill one day.

"Keep it and don't tell Mommy," George said.

After the feature, we'd stand at the exit gate—him on one side, me on the other—while the cars crawled by, looking for speakers still hanging on car windows, their cords dangling alongside the doors. We'd pound on the windows to get them back. Often the drivers would just ignore us, which would piss George off mightily. I watched him several times jump on the back bumper of a miscreant vehicle, bouncing hell out of it like he were some gone-amuck chimpanzee. "Goddamnit, those speakers ain't included in the price of admission!" he'd exclaim.

He remembered this Studebaker sedan with two couples in it who'd ignored him and went off with one of the speakers. Well, two nights later the same car showed up, same males but with two different women. George waited until the movie got started. Then went up and banged hard on the passenger door where the lady was sitting. She opened up, and he grabbed the speaker off the window. Just stood there staring at the driver. The man jumped out of the car and told him to give the girl back the fucking speaker.

"You got your own," George calmly answered. "Use it."

The driver threatened to beat the shit out of him.

It was then I saw George's gun. A silver Derringer. He calmly pulled it out of his pants pocket and held it discreetly down by his groin, so the ladies couldn't look at it. But the driver did. Who subsequently got back in his car. They sat there, all quiet-like staring at the screen for a while, George holding the speaker through which voices were coming. The driver within minutes started the vehicle and sped out of the theater.

"Ask me where I learned how to do that."

"Where, Uncle George?"

"*Alcatraz!*" And he reached out grabbing my arm and kneaded the bone. "Nobody fucks with old Uncle George. Do ya give up?"

We walked over to the concession stand. "Dinner for two. My boy, Westley, and me. And plenty of gravy!" The attendant took two frankfurters, split them lengthwise, placed them on a slice of sandwich bread, squirted mustard all over them until they were no longer visible, then slapped another slice of bread on top. He deftly cut each into triangular halves, and with a big handful of popcorn, served to us on a paper plate. And asked what we were drinking.

"Two doubles," George answered.

Reaching into the container of ice cream, the concessionaire placed two scoops into separate cups, and poured cherry soda up to its rim. "Anything else, Georgie-boy?"

"No thank you, Sam."

"What kind of a panty-night do you think it will be this evening?"

George looked up at the screen and saw Edward G. Robinson. "At its best, three and they will all be size forty or better."

Min's pancakes never did get baked, like the pie. For some goddamn reason she only made them at my house back in Hebron.

\* \* \*

But in just under a week I could see her putting the pressure on Uncle George to have me move on. He and I were spending too much time together. Making plans about going up to Pymatooming Dam to fish overnight in a couple of days. And we were pooling the money we found on the theater's gravel floor for fishing supplies: bait and tackle and bobbers. George had rigged me up a tackle box he'd found in the drive-in's supply shed and shared with me some basic fishing gear out of his box. It had become my prized possession. Each morning while waiting for him, I'd look inside the box and examine the lures he gave me like they were jewels handed down from mother to daughter. Earrings, things like that.

Jesus Christ, but he was a nice man. And went to Leavenworth Penitentiary in Kansas even. Knowing him like I did now, in a kind of perverse way I was proud of him for having done that. I wanted badly to ask him about it, but I'd been sworn to secrecy by my father. If he'd a gone to college, he sure as hell would have told me. Just to think about it pisses me off. Min too, I am certain, warned him direly if he ever let on.

Shit. What a waste.

And for him to have stolen a cucumber from its commissary on the way out says to me they sure as hell didn't take a nick out of his spirit.

But she was winning. And the last morning of my stay, George asked me to drive over to Mrs. Nelson's big bakery with him to load up on day-old bread. Seems Min was selling it for a small profit to some of the Skyline regulars she'd made acquaintance with. Once out of the Skyline grounds, George spoke:

"Westley, I won't be seeing you anymore until I come back to Hebron."

I knew it was coming. And Christ, felt all hurt. I really wanted to crawl up in the little back seat of the coupe where I had been sleeping each night and damn near die.

"What is it, Uncle George?"

He grabbed my arm and kneaded it real hard. Almost to the point of making me cry . . . which I wanted to anyway. Then he blurted out, "Do you give up?"

"YES!" I sighed.

"Goddamnit, so do I," he said. "Fucking Mommy. You and me, we've been having too much fun. She wants me back there in that coffee-can of a home with her. So I can watch her shoe polish her hair and nail polish her toes. And eat canned hash with forks containing food webs. But I ain't got no choice now, son. Mommy and me go way back. Clear to *ALCATRAZ*." And he laughed ironically. Reached into his pants pocket and palmed his Derringer and slid it across the front seat to me.

"It's yours, boy. In all its phony, fake glory. But use it like you think it's real. If you do it right, you don't have to be scared of any sonofabitch who's trying to take advantage of you.

"Use it like I taught you. Not for bad things, mind you. Nope. Uncle George never would do that. You don't frighten women with it either. It's . . . shall we say . . . a piece of JUSTICE you'll be carrying around in your pants.

"Use it discriminately. And I promise you, nothing will ever frighten you again.

"Not even MOMMY in the middle of the night."

And once more he reached over as if he were going to grab my arm and knead it. But he didn't. Instead he embraced me like no man had ever done before. And, Jesus, it felt better than all my imaginings about bein' folded up, suffocating, in Min's flesh. He and I sat there for the goddamnedest longest time starin' out the window, watching the cars speed by on Trumbull County Highway. And no big screen in front of us.

"You got any good ponds in Hebron?" he asked.

"One up the street. The Croton quarry. But I don't know whether it got any fish in it?"

"What do you and me care?" he responded. "Do you plan on going back home?"

"I don't know," I answered.

"Where might you be headed?"

"I ain't figured out just yet."

"Well, keep me informed with a postcard or something, huh?"
I nodded.

"Keep a look out for ponds. I don't care where you end up. Fuck it, even in Kansas. I'll go back there if I have to, just to fish with you."

"What about Min?"

He made a snorting noise.

"We ain't much longer on this earth. What the hell could she do to me if I slipped off for a few days? Let me worry about that. You just drop me a line. And I'll sneak out that night. She knows how to clean the shit out of the theater.

"Soon we be closing it up for the boss anyway when it gets cold. Ain't a damn thing to do when it shuts down. Mighty bleak when it snows, I'll tell you, and the screen is dark night after night for months at a time. The snow piles up to the speakers. And not a damn soul in sight. Me and her in that fucking upturned washtub back in the rear. Who ever knows we're alive? And I just sit there at our table while she lies in bed all day with shoe polish and curlers in her hair. And we're keepin' warm by a small kerosene stove. Jesus, how many games of solitaire can you play? So you drop me a postcard, do you hear?"

And this time he grabbed the arm and kneaded it like before.

*"Do you give up, huh?"* he whispered.

# THE AVIARY

**W**ESTLEY AND ME were like two lovers, who, for some mysterious reason, couldn't get it together. Something in the other always caused bad memories.

Take Evelyn. Started shaking when she was forty. Mother, Christina and Ethel, her sisters, talked non-stop about Evy's condition. We'd go up and visit, Westley, Mother and me. She'd greet us at the front porch, her house dress buttoned lopsided and her cranium shaking like she had a washing machine motor inside agitating it. She'd be grinning yes, but her head jerked no, and every now and then java saliva would vein across her chin. We'd watch her shuffle through the shade-drawn rooms toward the cluttered kitchen like somebody twice her age, grabbing onto chair backs, brass floor lamps, sliding against the water-stained papered walls to steady herself. At her dinette table she'd begin speaking, and I'd look up at her thinking, *Jesus, where in the hell's the switch?*

She needs for somebody to find that switch. She's standing in the Fun House at Idora Park on one of those vibrator pads that shake your teeth, and when you try to speak, spittle shoots out at your friends. Aunt Evelyn's one of those wooden toy puppets on a paddle dancing to somebody's terrible joke.

My mother spoke to a doctor in Cleveland. He said he'd drill into Evelyn's head, sever a nerve and the shaking would cease. Just like that. So all of us were very happy. We could now relax and look her in the eyes. The doctor was going to shut off that torturous tumbler. Once again she would speak like the rest of us with noth- ing sloshing out her mouth onto her soiled shift. She wouldn't look like an inmate in the county sanitarium any longer. Because she was my favorite aunt. And no longer any fun to be around.

Mother accompanied her to the Cleveland clinic for the proce- dure, nursed her there for two weeks, then brought her back home by Trailways. I'd inquire how Aunt Evelyn was getting along. "Is she up and around now, Ma? Is she washing and ironing again? How soon can she drive the car and come up and visit us?"

"Be awhile longer," Mother said.

Several weeks after the operation, I happened to come home early from school and saw Mother getting into our car. "Where you going?" I asked.

"To see Evelyn."

"Can I come?"

"I suppose," she answered.

At Evelyn's house it was always customary to knock and wait. But this time we walked right in. A stale, musty odor hung in the living room as dense as its shadows. Out at the old table sat Evelyn, staring over her backyard, the afternoon sunlight lying like a warm puddle on top the oil cloth cover.

"Evy, it's Margaret and James." We stood at the sink board wait- ing for her to acknowledge our presence. "Evelyn, I've brought you some soup." Like we weren't there. Mother sat down alongside her and placed her arm about my aunt's body. I stood in wonderment, watching the two sisters, one softly ministering, the other locked in a vacant conversation with something out in the willow tree, now both of them shaking bells whose clappers had disappeared.

Shortly she asked me to fetch Aunt Evelyn a spoon, then pro- ceeded to pour shellfuls of hot broth into her open mouth. But I saw a *beak*. For both these sisters now looked to me like rarified birds, a mother bird feeding a crippled bird. The latter's eyes caught in a quizzical glare, dumb to utter any reasonable sounds it once knew, only erratic squawks while attempting with all its energy to lift its bony talon off the warm oil cloth to shakingly, now in massive, explosive arcs, point at the *thing* she sees in the willow tree. That *person* to whom Mother and I are oblivious.

Evelyn's body in a coffin didn't frighten me nearly half as much as that final visit. Her house, which had long been a repository of good memories, a happy place where Westley and I always wanted to go on Sunday, preceded her in death that day. The willow tree secreted a stranger whom she clearly saw. Instead, her arm flapped about in the stale kitchen air like a swallow tethered to the table leg. Evelyn screeched and squawked, the saliva and warm chicken broth now rising rapidly inside her jaw trap, spouting over its outside accompanied by the unseemly odor of a vinegary urine rising up from somewhere under our chairs.

# THE PRUNER

THE FIRST TIME I saw him, Mother was down in the cellar washing clothes. A knock came at the door and this rugged old man in a pair of black suit pants, a suit vest, and a white shirt buttoned to the collar with no tie, asked if my father was home.

"No, he's at work," I said.

"How 'bout your mother?" The old man smiled red-eyed at me. He had bristly raven hair parted down the middle, a liver-spotted complexion, and no teeth. His hands looked like a boxer's, square.

"*Jake!*" Mother exclaimed, tugging at her apron. "Joe's not here. Was he 'specting you?"

The visitor turned and pointed to the single tree in our backyard, a knotted antique apple tree. "It will give you a better harvest if you let me tend to it."

"Jake . . . why, sure," she said.

"Joey wouldn't mind. Can I borrow a saw?"

"James, run down to the cellar and get the saw."

Soon Jake was climbing up into the twisted branches of the great apple tree with our dull handsaw hanging off his old leather belt like a scabbard. He shimmied, pulled, and swung his way to the very top. For the rest of the morning and that afternoon he worked his way back down, never once stopping to either accept Mother's offer of a bologna sandwich or the bathroom.

"*It's your grandfather,*" she whispered.

I was dumbfounded. "What's he doing here?"

"God only knows. Probably down at the corner saloon then wandered up here. I just hope your father gets home before he's done," she said. "*What am I supposed to do when he climbs back down?*"

I went upstairs and observed him from my bedroom window. How facile, this seventy-five-year-old moving through its tortured branches. Now and then he'd smear his brow with his yellowing dress-shirt sleeve. Earlier at the door I didn't smell whiskey, but a sweet and rancid odor rose off his stooped frame.

Before Father came home from work, Jake knocked on the door again. Even I could tell he'd taken off too many of its branches.

"Katherine, you tell Joseph I'll finish the job first thing tomorrow morning." Smiling guilelessly at me, he waved to Mother who stood just inside our screen door. He was off and back down the road.

"Oh God, he's coming back tomorrow."

"Where's he going?" I asked.

"Back to Piesto's."

That night my father crashed about in the backyard asking what in God's name happened to the great apple tree, accusing me and my friends of having taken hatchets and saws to it. Mother quickly alerted him to Jake's visit.

"Jake! What was *he* doing here?" Father burst.

"He's coming back tomorrow, Joe."

"To do what! Trim the fucking doors?"

Actually I was impressed. I hadn't ever seen anyone work so diligently with the clarity and skill as to what my grandfather'd done. He might have killed the tree, but by God it no longer looked arthritic.

But Jake never showed.

That spring not one cluster of white buds or a single green leaf emerged from what by now'd been christened *Jake's Apple Tree.* Just a black-barked hulking sculpture stood spectrally out of our backyard. Mother twisted a silver eye hook into its trunk to which she tied one end of her clothesline, the other into the corner board of our house. Father had it chopped to the ground that winter.

I still clearly see agile old Jake slicing his woody foe to the damp ground below. The vanquisher in sodden black wool, beaming back at the house to me—a wondrous progenitor of my father, Circus Mark, Dancer Agnes, and Holy Father Ray. This creature with burled hands the age of the tree he just killed. *Why, Jesus, Mary, and Joseph, the bushel baskets of ripe apples lying under its newly trimmed bows next August!* Jake the steeplejack. Going from neighborhood to neighborhood hunting down his offspring. "*Tomorrow I'll visit Agnes. Then Mark. Why, Raymond must have a whole orchard backside the chancery. He can go fishing while I fly about in his trees,*" an old Jake-bird leaping from limb to limb with a dull handsaw and madness.

I hadn't the least idea where Jacob Daugherty was even buried.

# WHITE SHOULDERS

*W*HEN GRANDMOTHER AGNES passed away, Jake Daugherty stood over her casket before they snapped it shut, reached into the right-hand pocket of the black suit the mortician had rented him and pulled out his set of teeth. Agnes clutched the rosary beads in one hand across her heart. Grandfather placed his dentures in the other, positioning them over her breast. Father, Mother, my brother, Westley, and I circled the coffin, touched.

Two years later Westley passed away. Grace and he had recently purchased a house in a subdivision outside Toledo, Ohio, that six months earlier had been a beet farm. Heretofore strangers, Westley and several neighbors labored weekends to erect decks on the backs of each other's neo-colonial homes. Elaborate affairs, these summer conceits cantilevered over raw backyards with precipitous drop-offs. The cedar decks were half as large as the homes' interiors where the drywall mud bouquet still lingered. Three months into the project—his was next up on the list—following a Saturday morning's work of hammering deck joists into place, Westley swanned pearl-white through the open slider of his neighbor's house, complained of stomach cramps, then bent over and died.

At the closing-of-the-lid ceremony not a single family member was surprised when young Lucien, who's as tall as Grace, drew a sixteen-ounce claw hammer from under his suit jacket and pried open his father's hands.

"What in Christ's name are they gonna dump in my coffin?" Pap whispered.

Following the burial and feed at Westley's house—Grace and Mother had gone to bed—Father and I remained seated at the dining room table that groaned from the mourners' goodwill: two turkeys, a honey-baked ham, several Tupperware crocks of potato salad and coleslaw, baskets of rolls and cheese Danishes, a chocolate cake.

"Is it a celebration or a damn funeral?" Pap groused. We'd begun drinking in the hearse on the way to the cemetery, and he'd become a little ornery. "I mean look at all this crap. Did you hear them out there in the kitchen tonight, laughin' and swillin' Westley's last case of Rolling Rock, makin' plans to construct a colossal deck off the back-end of their East Jesus clubhouse in Wes' honor, memorializing it with a tombstone plaque? And Grace—did you notice how touched she was?"

"What could she say, Pap?"

"Young Lucien sitting next to the sink, darkening up, not saying a damn word. 'You bastards!' that's what he was thinking, James. 'If it weren't for all of you neighbors wantin' to be sittin' outside with your strawberry wives every night watchin' the sun dip into the beet farm and swattin' the damn mosquitoes off your fat asses on the deck my daddy helped build for you, he'd be sittin' here with us now. Fuck your memorial!' That's what he was thinking, wasn't he, James?"

"These people understand death, Pap. The boy's too young to grasp it."

"Well, how *do* you goddamn grasp it?"

Father was thinking maybe he was supposed to be next in line. But Westley beat the old man into the sod.

"Shit, it could be me," I said.

"I can feel it in my bones, it's me," he said, rising. He walked over to the missing deck's slider, staring down into the ravine. "Can I confess something to you?" he asked.

"Don't become all teary-eyed on me now," I laughed.

"Who am I supposed to tell—Margaret?"

Margaret was my mother and she stopped listening to him twenty years ago. He sliced a wedge of ham off its shank.

"Let me put that on a roll with some lettuce and mayonnaise for you, Pap."

"Goddamnit, *Junior* . . . now don't tell me how to eat!"

I sat back in the chair. The house was dead quiet. I kept picturing Westley floating in the periwinkle viewing room with his eyes glued shut and a prophylactic grin on his once-sweet face that froze to a mask of terror when he slipped to his knees. The Stanley framing hammer in his stiff hand, a rubber over its red handle for comfort gripping—the incongruity of it all. What would the anthropologists say when they unearthed King Westley Tutankhamen Daugherty's bier one millennium from now to confront a skeleton with a death grip on a claw hammer? And Agnes Daugherty several hundred yards away, clasping a set of uppers and lowers in one hand, rosary beads in another? When Johnny Prioletti, our neighbor, died, his widow tossed his Bobby Jones', a fresh deck of cards, and a bottle of Jim Beam into her stiff's canoe.

"Are you listening to me?" Pap said.

"Yes," I said. "Goddamnit, yes."

"Son, I can't get an erection anymore."

I just stared at him.

"You hear what I'm tellin' you? Used to be any excuse of the opposite sex, their legs, perfume, even passing the millinery shop on Washington Street, for Chrissake, it'd jump up—in confession, too, or when I damn near got drafted for World War II." He paused, chewing off more of the ham he held between his fingers. "Now I can't will the sonofabitch to raise its head. Even when I pet it." He grinned slyly.

"Oh, you're pulling my leg, goddamnit."

"It's how the Maker lets us know when we ain't got much time left, James. My friends all think I drop it into your mother at least twice a week. Ain't so. Her pussy's drier than an Okie dust bowl."

I turned out the light and headed toward the stairway.

"Oh, don't get so goddamn prissy!" he laughed, collegially embracing me, gently pushing me back into my chair. The moonlight cast an eerie, fluorescent pall over the food. "I'm just telllin' you like it is, boy. No tumbling weed even rolling through your mother's thing. It's a lunarscape, for Chrissake. Wouldn't matter anyway. 'Cause I've told you what's been ailing me: my dog won't raise its ornery head for love nor money. Tired, Son. Over. Kaput. *I'm an old man.*"

"Stop feeling sorry for yourself, Pap."

"Old man Nowles sure gussied Wes up good, didn't he? Huh? Christ, our boy looked like they colored his face with pastels. Say, you'll regret not taking the opportunity we got between us now. Listen to what I'm tellin' you, Son. And it ain't the booze talkin', goddamnit! Your pecker collapses on you like a five-and-dime card-table leg before your ticker *ever* gives out."

He was stretching to win me now.

"Let me ask you a personal question. I don't wish to offend you." He offered me a cigarette. "But we're friends, right?"

"Right."

"Dear friends."

"Uh-huh."

"Father and son, right? A team."

"Right."

"Some things you 'n me shared we couldn't with nobody else, right?"

"Right."

"Even with our loving wives, huh?" He slurred "loving."

"That's right," I said.

"Do you masturbate?"

"Oh, for Chrissake, Pap!"

"Well, of course you do. Now, how do you accompany yourself?"

"Accompany myself?"

"You goddamn well know what I mean, Jimmy."

"Enough of this shit. Let's go to bed."

"Pictures. The old head projectionist. You know ... what's sprocketing up in the old noggin." He sighed. "*What kind of pictures do you roll inside your fucking head when you're whacking off, James!*"

"I can't tell you."

"You sure you don't want a slice of this?" He jabbed at the ham. In the morning the women would throw it into the soup.

"Chiaroscuro, is that the word? Her shoes, the cheap jewelry she wore. And if I concentrated hard enough, I'd even get the picture show in my head to fabricate the fragrance she wore that evening. *White Shoulders.* Honest to Christ, I can still smell it.

"The reel would open in the back seat of my car, me unfastening her rayon blouse, it's catchin' the light in the evening sky like pond water, she's rollin' down hose over her dimpled knees and droppin' her tiny shoes into the driver's seat. Jesus. Both of us gettin' baby-ass naked. The car windows sweatin' and I ain't worryin' a damn about the battery dying, for the old Delco's red-lit in the dashboard playin' a Dorsey tune. Two trombones *waaa-waaaing* in the front seat and me 'n' her's about to do it in the back."

Father stood and walked into the doorway's grotto. I could barely make him out. Hand shadows glided painterly across Westley's empty walls.

"The perfume, Jimmy—like the projectionist up in my head poured some vials of efflorescence onto the sprockets—because as her body rose up to meet me, so did her earthly scent. Like I'd just spaded her. I coaxed her outside the automobile and shuddered watchin' the moon drop its cold shaft across her backside, then straddle her milky breasts. And when I pushed her down into the fresh loam, Jimmy, making our body bed, up in the old Delco, Dexter Gordon's wailing *Body and Soul*, accompanying our moanin', while the old farmer's sprocketing his dream upstairs in his iron bed—Son, it was all sorghum-sweet, sour and bittery bliss. Dexter's roller-coastin' low tones and squeals, the projectionist's clacking it all for eternity, and . . ."

Father slumped back into his chair. We were shadows now. He lit a cigarette. It arced back and forth across his argent face like a beat-farm firefly.

"God only knows how many times that single feature rolled upstairs in my bedroom, Jimmy. Down in East Jesus she strolled off with other lovers, but in that reel she remained fresh as her bloody perfume that muddy night. And your mother asleep downstairs."

The old man's voice grew plaintive now. Talking to himself in a hush. The light in the room unforgiving, the food on the table funereal. We should have been on a porch swing out in the meadow. Or in a Packard Phaeton alongside a metallic lake in Maine, for it felt like we were out sitting on one of Westley's new decks, the harsh light of suburbia baking down on us.

"James," he said.

"Yes, Pap. Go on."

"The silver nitrate's peeled off my celluloid, boy. It's gone bad in the can. I sprocket it up now, 'n all I get are shards, blank frames. She won't rise to the occasion. I coax, cajole. Then like life ascending out of a chemical bath . . . she begins to rise in a red light. Her breasts, I remember. The scar river runnin' indigo into and out of her navel. And the moon, a flickering headlamp, begins to trace her torso, stopping at her . . . but she slips back away from me, Jimmy! Back down into the cistern on the old man's farm. And the fucking static's killin' Dexter in our front seat, and my car's goddamn doors flappin' open like gills of a beached pickerel . . ."

"I want to go to bed, James."

"You are crying, Father."

He rubbed his face bemusedly. "By God . . . Huh? I'll be damned. I don't have any idea where they come from either."

"Pap . . . it's melancholia."

"Sad? Why? They buried your brother today with his claw hammer. What's so fucking melancholic about that? And you, I've got you, dear friend, sittin' next to me. In the old car. Listening to our radio. Lester Young . . . ," he said. "See if you can dial up the Prez, Son. And ask her if she's needin' anything."

"Who?"

"Genevieve, the young lady in the back seat. The woman with her legs crossed and smokin' Pall Malls. Is there anything she's wantin'?" He stood and wandered over to the sliders, staring down into the hollow.

"No, Pap. She's says she's all set."

"Me too," he said, turning in the shadows. "Let's be off then."

The light of the beet farm's sky cast its mirrory blade across his face as he stood there waiting for me to take his hand. I walked toward him, placed my arms tightly about his chest and squeezed hard. Then caught our reflection in the slider's glass.

Westley's, too.

# NOLDE'S SUN

*D*ECADES HAVE PASSED and I still don't understand why a sequence of events that occurred over a span of three weeks caused a sun that never sleeps to rise in my consciousness. To this day it continues to burn, perhaps not as bright, but it does cast its glow over all aspects of my daily routine. And the color of the sun is an Emile Nolde red. Like blood filtered through yolk. Luminescent, yet flesh-alive. As if it were a heart beating on the horizon that is shot through with a seraphic orange, an orange that erupts in the mind, curls off that star like fire hairs, and burns much of what the mind ingests to ash.

I mustn't get carried away. It's that damn Nolde sun. Let me attempt to explain. I reclined on our bungalow's porch one evening long ago in the company of my parents and their two best friends, Bernice and Thaddeus Richter, who had strolled up the hill from the house they occupied at the bottom of our street. Their daughter, Leila, two years older than me, babysat young Ben. Gently rocking on a swing secured to the porch's rafters by chains, I lay listening to the soft palaver of the adults. The four of them sat on the top step. My elementary school faced our house. It was my final year.

Soon wearying of their chatter, I concentrated instead on the celestial patterns the fireflies traced about me in the night air, when a distinct change in the timbre of the conversation occurred. The women's words began to bubble, interrupted by a nervous, high-pitched laughter; the men's voices sawed viola-like.

"Oh no, she wouldn't," I heard my father profess.

"That's how much you know about me," Mother answered.

"Tell him, Margaret," Bernice urged. "They think they know all there is to know about us. Just because we've undressed for them."

"It's always dark," Father said.

"You don't give me the pleasure often enough, Bernice," Mr. Richter chided.

"Well, maybe I just haven't any reason to."

Both women chortled. Mr. Richter lit a cigarette.

"Some men bring their wives flowers or gifts. Jake here brings home a satchel of the clothes he soils at the pottery each day. Sits down and asks 'What's for supper?' Pretty damn hard to get amorous about that."

"Same like Thaddeus, Margaret. Leaves for the foundry at 6:00 in the morning. Maybe not home before 7:00 at night. Smelling of flux and sulphur. Grease-covered like he were in a minstrel show. And he wants to lie on my white sheets that I've bleached and aired out in the sun. You men got to understand we ain't farm animals. We're bloomin' women ... and we like, in fact *enjoy*, being romanced from time to time. Ain't that right, Margaret?"

I heard no response until my father spoke up.

"Shit. Why didn't you both say so? If that's all it takes, I'll go upstairs right now, take a bath, and sprinkle some talc on my jewels. And if it's flowers you want, by Jesus, just you wait here."

They laughed. Jake loped around the side of the house, and I sat up on the swing. Momentarily he was back standing before the others in the middle of our sidewalk; he'd dropped his trousers, and there sticking out between his legs—a hollyhock stalk. The showy clusters glowed reddish purple in the wavering streetlight.

"Jake, what will the neighbors think, for God's sake!"

Mother dropped to her knees, tugging up his pants, still laughing, as were Bernice and Thaddeus. When my father sat back down, and the excitement evaporated, Mother absent-mindedly dropped her head onto his shoulder, cradling the heliotrope bouquet. Thaddeus draped an arm around Bernice. Soon the couples were dead silent. The fireflies now seemed more abundant.

Until laughter exploded in the street down near the McCart's house. Male and female laughter—there must have been several people who were raucously advancing. I sat up in the swing again.

"Jake, will you look at that?" Thaddeus enthused.

"There, Margaret. That's what you and Bernice talked about," Father crowed.

"Where do you think they're headed to?" Bernice asked.

"Out to Cascade Park. A pack of dogs following the bitch's scent—whadaya expect?"

"Two women, four men," Thaddeus corrected.

"OK, two bitches, Ted," Mother replied.

"Look at that one with the red hair, will you, Margaret? Do you think they'll ever get there in time?" Bernice giggled.

The auburn-haired girl, perhaps eighteen, was dressed in a Turkey-red summer shift, dropped low at the bodice. A sooty rouge caused her cheeks to cup unnaturally in the scarce light. She strolled with a cool insolence while two buzz-cut males swaggered at her sides. They were all strangers to our street. The other female, a wispy blond, hung back and appeared to be lost in thought. The young men in tow smoked jerkily.

We watched them wander up the street where they stopped directly under the streetlight. The redhead tossed a paper sack onto Miss Gresham's, our music teacher's, lawn, then erupted with the others in a communal hoot before disappearing into the dark.

"Westley, go get that bag. See what it is she dropped," Mother said.

"Oh for Chrissake, Margaret, don't tell the kid to do that. God knows what's in it."

"Go ahead, Westley."

I dutifully fetched the bag and handed it to Mother. The adults all huddled to see what it contained.

Mother began to open it, then stopped. "You do it, Bernice."

"Give it to Ted," Bernice said. "He's seen everything, haven't you, Honey?"

Thaddeus Richter, without responding, took the bag from Mother and opened it. His head twitched backward.

"Whew!" He tossed the bag out into our lawn.

"Oh my God! Can you believe it, Margaret?" Bernice cried.

Mr. Richter spit into the grass.

"What a little whore. Oh, Jesus!" Mother exclaimed. Both women jumped up, brushing their chests as if a toxic powder had laced their garments. They waddled about in a choreographed dance of disgust. The men just howled.

"What was it?" I asked.

Nobody answered.

"Tell me. I want to know." Still no response.

I bounded off the porch to retrieve the bag, but was summarily collared by my father. "Go back up on the swing, Son. Or go to bed. It's something adult."

"Well, how's she going to give those *whoresons* what they're panting for if she's got the curse, Margaret?" Bernice asked.

"The bitch's in heat," Mother huffed. "I certainly wouldn't."

Both men snickered when Father said something to the effect that he "mightn't be Casanova, but he damn well sure wasn't a bloodhound, either."

"Let's follow them," Mother said.

"I'm game," Mr. Richter answered.

"You want to come, Westley?" Father asked.

"Oh, Jake," Mother scolded.

"He fetched the sack for you, didn't he?"

"He's only a kid."

"That's how much you know," Father said. "How else is he to find out? You going to tell him?"

"Well, it's for damn sure he ain't going to learn it from you . . . sticking gladioli between your legs."

"Weren't no gladioli, Margaret," Bernice softly intoned.

We all piled into our '36 Dodge sedan with Father taking the wheel, heading out to Cascade Park. By then I knew our journey had something to do with sex. It was a taboo subject, and I only sensed it because it left a strange but powerful smoldering at the drop of my spine. I felt at once nauseated and stimulated. Like Nolde's sun had begun to rise in my groin. Of course I didn't know that then.

The adults scanned the roadside. Mother suggested that Father turn off the headlights.

"There they are!" shouted Bernice.

Sitting up on a hillside overlooking the park's garishly lit entrance, the revelers shared a smoke. It passed among them like a firefly. I could barely make out their shadowy forms. The Jackrabbit plunged metallically into the gorge below to the delight of the amusement park's evening riders.

"They've finished," Father said.

"I'm not surprised," Mother replied.

It was an anticlimax for sure. The parents taking me on this little excursion to witness what adults do in the dark. (And that mysterious bag.) But the revelers only shared a cigarette, leaning detached against a mighty oak. As we drove the Richters home, words flitted about in the cloth-lined automobile much the same as yesterday, not going anywhere, a palpable, post-coital air hanging stale in our sedan.

Leila's light was still on.

\* \* \*

The following Monday, from my arithmetic class, I saw Mother suddenly appear on our front porch looking distraught, then rush down off the steps heading straight for the school.

"Westley, take your seat, please!" Mrs. Robbins shot up from her desk in the back of the room.

"Westley, come home immediately." Of no mind to explain her urgency, Mother waved me out of the classroom. "You play in the woods across from the Richters' house," she ejaculated, dragging me down the schoolhouse steps. "Maybe you know where he might be hiding."

"Tell me what's wrong, Ma!"

"Little Ben's wandered out of his backyard this morning while Bernice was hanging out the wash. He's been missing over an hour, and I fear the worst."

We raced down the hill. Ben was three years old, redheaded, and—unlike his laconic father—adventurous. He was always getting into some kind of trouble, "a handful" as Bernice described him. A week earlier he'd gotten lodged behind their claw-footed bathtub, his legs twisted around its hot and cold water pipes. Greasing the boy's legs with Vaseline, Mr. Richter pulled and tugged. Finally he shut off the water and hacksawed laughing Ben free. This day Bernice had disappeared into the cellar to retrieve another basket of wet laundry. Ben sat playing trucks in the sandbox.

In the pucker brush and alder across the street from the Richters', my friends and I'd built a camp out of screen doors salvaged when the grade-school bought new aluminum ones. I'd told young Ben about taking him to our secret camp one day. I said it was a long hike and he and I would pack a lunch and go on this journey into the woods.

"Ben keeps talking about going to 'Westley's camp,'" Bernice said whenever she saw me. "He wants me to pack him a lunch like I do for Thaddeus each morning," she'd erupt in a watery laugh, patting me on the shoulder. "'When is Westley coming down, Mom,'" he badgers.

"You're such a good friend to him, Westley. He thinks you're his brother."

* * *

I liked the kid, especially his irrepressible spirit. Everything else was always too perfect in the Richters' household for me. Thaddeus had a good welding trade, working on all the semi-trailer rigs and large stamping machinery over at the tin mill. A Steinway sat in their living room for Leila to play, and every year Thaddeus went out and bought a top-of-the-line Chrysler station wagon for Bernice, indigo blue. She also kept crystal bowls freshly supplied with cellophane-wrapped candies on her end tables.

"White Shoulders," Mother answered when I inquired what kind of perfume Bernice wore. I'd watch her primping inside her bedroom suite (separated from the rest of the house by French doors)—a Turkish towel wrapped about her head and garmented in a thick terrycloth robe, dabbing a glass stopper to her neck and bare legs. I was used to smelling soap powder, or occasionally pie flour on Mother. Bernice Richter smelled like I thought a woman was meant to smell.

I know my father was attracted to her.

In our camp I didn't find Ben. A galvanized culvert, in which a grown man could stand, snaked behind and down a gully several hundred yards long. I walked into the pipe until the circle of light behind me closed.

"Ben! Ben Richter!"

*Ben! Ben Richter!* the echo.

Hurrying back out of the woods, I saw Mother loping down our dirt road that had been freshly oiled by the sprinkler trucks that morning. Her shoes were sticking to its surface. She screamed as if she were on fire.

*"Ben's dead! Little Ben's dead!"*

The neighbor women all rushed off their porches. Summoned the minute Ben'd been discovered lost, Thaddeus Richter was out scouring the neighborhood with Father at his side. Bernice lay caterwauling in her shuttered bedroom while Mrs. Gee, her backyard neighbor, applied cold washcloths to her forehead. Mother had become unstrung when Leila began punching dissonant chords into the baby grand.

I ran up towards the steel mill. The foundry, located at the edge of the neighborhood, broadcast a grating metallic din day and night. In a supply yard surrounding the complex lay a farm pond, a frothy slime bubbling up on its surface smelling of methane—a biting sulfurous odor. Ben lay face-down in the green liquid, his arms languidly out to his sides in a dead man's float, darning needles flitting about his head. Mr. Richter held a two-by-four in his hands, and, betraying no emotion, mechanically oared the boy back to land. My father stood staring off into the red horizon.

Once I'd watched Thaddeus weld a fender that had come unhinged from the body of a neighbor's Chevrolet. An intense concentration mapped his expressionless face. The only thing missing here was the spark. The flame from the torch. Nolde's sun.

By now the acid bath had caused Ben's carrot-red hair to stand in marked contrast to his jaundiced complexion and rayon sun suit. Mr. Richter pressed his son's head to his breast. I could smell Ben. His scent was that of a dud firecracker, an ignited one spiked into the black earth, impotently spewing a sulfurous phlegm into the air.

The bilious liquid dripped as the two men walked grimly toward the fence. Thaddeus crawled under and on the other side retrieved Ben from Father's arms. I walked down the freshly tarred road behind the pair. Not a word passed between them. It was a somber parade, Father walking ramrod stiff next to Thaddeus Richter, whose dark blue work shirt now turned lemon-yellow about young Ben's body. Neighbors gathered reverently on the side of the road, some quietly sobbing. The two fathers marched stalwartly, me tagging behind, until the cold procession halted at the Richters' lawn.

"Bernice! Oh God, Bernice," Thaddeus shouted. "Look what I'm bringing home. *Bernice!*"

I lay down on the grass bank and wept. In the house I could hear yowling women inveighing God to answer. Mr. Richter appeared dazed. The indigo-blue shirt with the mechanical pencils in his breast pocket had begun to decompose, melt like it were on fire. Nolde's fire. Father gestured to Mr. Gee and the other men to give assistance. They encircled Thaddeus, closing in on father and son, grasping each other by the elbow as if not to fall—like pallbearers. Up the Richters' banks they trudged in a solemn flank, inexorably, now as one. My father turned the crystal knob on the French doors, gesturing for the cortège to disappear into the house of screams.

\* \* \*

Ben Richter's drowning that day killed the innocence on Cascade Street. There would be no more adults snickering on porch steps after dark. My friends and I abandoned our camp. No desire to lie inside its screen-door enclosure late afternoons gazing though the canopy of alder leaves into a hemorrhaging twilit sky. Our dreams had all dissolved in young Ben's corrosive bath. Bernice Richter, once she recovered (it took over a year for her to regain her senses), now sent her laundry out. And for reasons I never understood until much later, Mother ceased being her friend. We moved to the west side of town.

\* \* \*

"You aren't man enough to admit it, that's all."

Having returned from yet another night of drinking and carousing with his friends, Jake sat across the kitchen table, glaring at Mother.

"Wipe that shit-eating grin off your face!" she cried.

Father sat remarkably stiff.

"Why don't you just say it after all these years?"

"It ain't right to condemn a good woman, Margaret." He was taking drunken umbrage.

"She was innocent as you pretend to be."

"I ain't innocent."

"No, and it's goddamn right that adulteress weren't either."

"Bernice Richter is no whore, Margaret."

"You slept with her, didn't you?"

Father tenaciously shook his head.

"You lie through your teeth!" Reaching behind, she grabbed the dish of stew she'd kept warming on the stove, hurling it across the Formica table. It shattered, bleeding umber rivulets down the buttercup wallpaper.

Father sat stoically.

"It was happening all along, wasn't it, and both of you made fools of me and Thaddeus. He was blinkered, too."

"Weren't nothing to know, Margaret."

"Bullshit you say. That's why Ben was taken away, *wasn't it, Jake?*"

Father, appearing alarmed—pricked out of his sardonic stupor—jumped up and drew back his arm as if to strike her. I moved out of the shadows of the dining room.

"What's going on?" I said.

He slid back into his chair.

"Your father was going to hit me, Westley."

"I weren't," he said soberly.

"You were about to strike me."

"I ain't ever hit a woman."

"But you screw them, don't you, Jake?"

"Only you, my love."

She spat on his shoes. "Tell Westley the awful truth, Jacob Daugherty!"

"Weren't no awful truth."

As if to muster the resolve, she braced herself against the porcelain stove. "Is it you want me to say, then?"

"Go right ahead, Margaret." He swung his chair about, eyeing me and her defiantly. "It's about Ben Richter, Westley," she said.

"What about him?" I asked.

"He's . . ."

Steadying himself against the table, Father stiffly rose: "He's your dead brother, Son," watching his dinner slide down the kitchen wall.

\* \* \*

Mother fell back into the chair, spent. A supercilious grin melting her grimace as she clasped my hand . . . just as she'd done the day of Ben's funeral. They'd attired him in a yellow suit identical to the one he wore floating in the pond, the one that began to melt away before our very eyes on the procession down Cascade Street. Like Nolde's sun were dissolving it. And by some cosmetic miracle, the undertaker, Joshua Reynolds, had made young Ben's body lose its sallow shade. It looked almost natural again, but . . . yes, as if he'd dabbed leg paint on it. He'd rouged Ben's lips, too. They were anthracite-black on Jake's and Thaddeus' parade. Mother drew me into the glow nimbusing Ben's body, reflecting off his satin coverlet and rising out of the throats of the heliotrope gladiolus tipping his hair. She clasped my hand, lifting it up over the casket's rim, to deposit it on Ben's stomach.

"Press, Westley," she said. "Go on, press. Don't be afraid," she said piously.

I pressed and felt stone. Ben was hard as granite. I drew my hand away in shock and looked to her for some explanation. She dropped her eyes, seductively, just as she had that evening long ago when the four of them invited me on that ride in the family sedan, and we turned our headlights off, heading east towards Cascade Park.

# CLOTH

*I*'VE NEVER UNDRESSED my wife.

Not once have I seen her step out of the bath, climb into a bathing suit, or crawl into our bed unclothed. I can draw her body with my hands. Every dimple, mole, collapse and bulge. In the dark, I see by touch. I know the terrain of her body better than I do my own. Place me in a room absent of light, permit me to touch the faces of five women—unerringly I'd pick Gabrielle's. My own face among four others, I'd fail the test.

It hasn't been her choice. I've heard some men complain their wives have never appeared before them nude. Gabrielle would express no such reserve. The conditions are mine. Even our wedding night, I insisted her body be absent illumination. My hands store that memory.

Why?

Father's woman danced nude. I saw her only unclothed and in a turkey trot. Always after everybody had gone to bed. James, my brother, and I'd be awakened by a shrill voice trailing back and forth in the upstairs hallway. Stark naked, she would be twirling and gesturing to her closed bedroom door, spitting out Father's name. At a Tabernacle Church in our neighborhood I'd witnessed women dancing in the aisles, speaking in tongues as if in a trance, to collapse exhausted onto the floor and shiver paroxysmally.

Father's woman danced like that, too. But hers was more a dance of curse. Vituperating him who lay awake on the other side of their bedroom door. She'd dip and stride, jump and twirl, point at the hallway light and cry, "You bastard! Tonight, I will jump off the Cement Dam. None of you believe it. But I will show each of you." Young James would begin crying. I'd tell him to be quiet, and that if she tried to leave the house, we'd follow her.

"She got to jig it out of her system. It's like the Holy Rollers "Strip the Willow." They foam at the mouth and collapse. She will, too, back in Father's bed. Nothing's going to happen. Now stop your damn bawling."

Mother lived in the same house, too. Just the four of us. But she never high-kicked, and I suspect Father never saw *her* naked either. Not that he didn't want to. He loved women, all kinds of women. A light turned on inside of him when the subject was raised. But not with Mother. Profoundly religious, and clothed tight to her cervix and far below her knees. Black-laced matron's heels. Hair in a netted bun pulled severely off her forehead, and no makeup—white as the flour she'd crank through her sifter daily. Mother'd chastise Father, James, and me for wandering through the house in a state of undress. "It's not proper!" she'd cry, running to fetch a shirt or a pair of trousers. James and I figured when we died, Jesus would greet us in a suit and tie. That's why they'd bury us so, too. Only the naked go to hell.

Mother wasn't doing the hysteria shuffle at two a.m. It was Lee Ann Daugherty. Curiously enough it was the first time James or I ever saw a naked woman. There had been pornographic depictions of women in literature down at the local gas station. Artists' renditions on men's rooms walls. But Lee Ann caterwauling back and forth in the hallway was our introduction to how the opposite sex actually looked indecently exposed. It wasn't pretty.

Threatening suicide off the Cement Dam that lay a mile up our road, 150-foot concrete wall that once held back the mighty Neshannock River. But decades earlier the Army Corps of Engineers diverted the river, and the Cement Dam now sat out there incongruous in the Hebron countryside, a barrier towering up inside a gorge. Wasn't a year go by that one or two citizens didn't take their life by leaping off it into the water-less rubble below. Townspeople began to believe it held persuasive powers, the whole terrain about the land, that if you ventured anywhere near, say even a half-mile, its elegiac pull would draw you to the dam and certain death. Even the utterance of the name frightened the youth of Hebron. *Satan* paled in power.

Lee Ann thrust its spell into us over her gavotte. Her swooping against the stained and unraveling wallpaper, darting like a moth against the door to our room. Her sobbing an ineluctable grief . . . for what, James nor I were ever certain. Her raw anger directed at Father and even, it appeared, at God. Why had either of them violated her so?

The coda to her lament: "You'll see. The whole damn bunch of you will see. I'm off to *Cement Dam*."

But she never went. Over time Lee Ann would wind down, her sobbing would grow less impassioned, her invectives against the closed door of Father's room fewer. Until finally, folding into a woman-ball, she rolled into a corner. Unmoving. No more wails, screeches, imprecations or threats. Shortly Father's door opened. "It's time to come to bed, dear," bending low to grasp Lee Ann's hand. Together they'd glide back into the dark, shutting their door softly.

Bright the next morning, Mother would appear. Her house dress buttoned to her sternum and skirting her calves. A pair of white sheer anklets and string-laced ward shoes. Wearing a gossamer hair net. (Lee Ann's hair fell to the swale in her back, barely touching her buttocks.)

James and I'd lie frigid in our bed following such performances, listening for any noise we might decipher. Grateful for the peace. Grateful that the dance would not erupt for another month. Grateful that we didn't have to follow her to Cement Dam. We'd offer a prayer, whispering it between ourselves. "Thank you, God. Lee Ann has flown our house once again. And could You keep her away longer next time?"

\* \* \*

Perhaps if we'd been youngsters at the time of the dithyrambs, say five or six years old, they wouldn't have affected us as they did much later. Lee Ann's flings, however provocative . . . it was the fact that she associated them with death that queered our vicarious pleasure. Sex, certainly—her out there springing her body off the mahogany-woodwork hallway in the flickering overhead light, the slapping of her bare feet onto the dark shellacked floors, her wailing and moaning, a larger-than-life shadowgraph billowing across the *fleur-de-lis* wallpaper. Hair moving rope-like about her naked torso, lashing and caressing it, a salt-and-pepper hawser. The fleshy mouth out of which lamentations shaped into mournful entreaties to God and Father. As if a plunge from 150 feet into Abraham's water-less bosom could be the only succor up to the task.

If this was sex, we were aroused and stricken by it. Father related to both women with characteristic equanimity, however.

Until the day Lee Ann became Mother.

\* \* \*

The early morning *danse du ventres* occurred with such predictable frequency for two years that eventually neither James nor I'd leap out of bed at their onset. We'd lie listening to Lee Ann's shrieking and body slump, awaiting Father's soothing voice, cajoling her back into their bed—caressing the door shut. Our prayers of relief had grown perfunctory. We were being lulled into the belief that Lee Ann would never carry out the *Cement Dam* threat.

Then James and I found employment working for a commissary at a nearby "Double A" ballpark. Three summer nights a week with a double-header on Sunday, several hundred Hebron citizens would pay to watch baseball. He worked the stands with a hot dog dispenser while I managed the refreshment booth. An August evening I was icing vendors' soda buckets when Father appeared at the admittance gate, summoning me out to the parking lot.

"Seems you better get home, Westley."

"Why?"

"It's your mother."

"What's wrong with her?"

"Well, nothing yet. But I just think you should stick around the house."

"I don't understand. What's wrong?"

"Like I said, nothing's wrong . . . yet. I don't like the way she's acting."

"Lee Ann, Dad?"

He shook his head. "She ain't showed for some time. Now your mother's begun talking just like her. I don't like it."

"Where are you going?"

"Out. You go on home now and be the man. You're old enough."

He climbed into his '36 Dodge sedan and drove off. An ominous cloud of gravel dust in his trail. I took off right behind him on my bicycle. When I entered the house I called out her name.

"Ma," I hollered. "Ma, where are you?" No answer. Maybe she's Lee Ann upstairs, fandangoing through our empty bedrooms. Is that what he meant? Or perhaps she was balled up like tumbleweed in the corner of our hallway. And he couldn't get her to stand up to go back into the bedroom. He spoke about my being a man now. It's what men do—grab their Lee Anns by the arms when they get this way, and lead them back into the confines of the dark bedroom they share. In the morning they exit as the real people we know. The people who don't dance to frighten.

Upstairs I could smell the cologne Father'd sprinkled on his body like he always did when we went out of an evening. I saw the imprint of a body on the counterpane in their room, perhaps Lee Ann's. Though Mother's string shoes sat neatly paired at the foot of the bed.

"Mother!" The sound ricocheted through the half-light bungalow. The only noise our refrigerator's dull drone.

The cellar, perhaps. Hanging up clothes on the lines strung overhead. She's ironing down there and didn't hear me. But as I ran downstairs and entered the kitchen . . . I froze. *Did I want to go down there?* Bad things always happen in basements. Rarely in one's living or dining room. The heinous acts always occur in that raw, undomesticated chamber of the house.

"Mother? Are you down there?" Father's face—why had he alerted me? What had she done, causing him to shift this time and never before?

At the base of the cellar steps sat a two-burner cast-iron gas grill on cement blocks. It was attached to the main gas feed by a terracotta-red rubber hose. Each summer Mother placed large blue porcelain kettles filled with newly picked tomatoes on its starfish burners. For hours the fruit would simmer into a sauce she'd jar and store for winter meals. The red pulp steaming, bubbling lava-like, popping and spitting red juice onto the white-washed cellar walls. Both porcelain cocks open wide.

She sat limp on a metal stool before the unlit stove, her head and arms buried beneath a chrysanthemum print washing machine cozy. A salmon-shaded chemise stopped at her knees. Bare legs and feet dangled at the sides of the stool.

Alongside lay a crumpled "Till Death Do Us Part" note, addressed to Father and signed by Mother's closest friend.

Caterwauling like Lee Ann, I gathered her in my arms and carried her out of the cellar, begging that she come alive. Her hair fell loose, brushing against my body each step I took. She felt cold. I cursed my departed father, cursed God, and begged that she not leave me alone.

*Gone to Cement Dam in James's and my absence.* And now I bore her body through the light-dying house, wailing. But nobody heard. I laid her on the sofa, thrust each of the windows open to the evening air—then pumped her chest as if I'd lifted her out of a pond. Calling her to make a sound, any sound, even if she'd speak in tongues . . . Oh, God . . . It would be sufficient.

"Please don't leave us!" Drumming her chest, her small frame bouncing ludicrously up and down on the mohair sofa cushions like a cloth doll. Father's woman. The *Lord-will-meet-us-in-the-hereafter-dressed-like-a-mannequin* woman. The *I-will-wear-my-faux-pearl-buttoned-chemise-with-black-patent-leather-shoes-and-purse-with-a-silver-clasp* woman . . . no Lee Anns allowed in the house of the Lord.

But I didn't want to be in the house of the Lord. My semi-nude headwater, the rise out of which I'd coiled fifteen years earlier, I willed to pull into the air, beat on her as they once beat on me and James—slapped us against the backside hard . . . before we bawled.

"Christ, Mother, come alive. Goddammit, come alive!" And in my mind I saw myself reaching into her balled-up soul, untangling her arms, and dancing her to the surface, watching her awake to gulp breath—suck the Hebron night air out of the gullies of all the cement dams of this world, God's fear-and-trembling threshers . . . and ever so fragile, a smile eddied her purple-rose lips.

Me on top of her like I'd ridden my ghost across the mesa of time.

"What did you do that for?" she asked.

For which I'd no answer.

# OH, JOSEPHINE

**N**OBODY COULD ANSWER with any degree of certainty why Buddy Hart did it. Twenty years old, hayseed-white with a libido laugh, a rhythm-and-blues keyboardist who owned a steady gig at the Hi-way Roller Dome on the Hammond B3 five nights a week, then crossed over to piano at the Bluebird where Cleveland's black jazz aficionados gathered on weekends. Even drove an indigo wood 'n' steel Chrysler Town and Country convertible without missing a payment.

But Buddy Hart felt branded.

He lived just above the Chesapeake and Ohio switching yard in East Niles. Municipal plumbing stopped one mile west in Danville, and the drains from his house and each of his neighbors' emptied into an open gutter alongside DeForest Road. Across the tracks sat a block of inconspicuous, soot-impregnated bungalows, the site of Ohio's more notorious cathouses. Buddy's mother and grandmother ran the cleaning concession.

The prodigy came by his talent mysteriously—at the age of five sat down at the Gospel Tabernacle upright in Bible School and began belting out facsimiles of "Bo Weevil" and "Walking To New Orleans" . . . Fats Domino tunes. Rupert, his old man, announced that Buddy was the "Hart's ticket out of East Niles," and the following Monday had an old Kimball with a few ivories missing proudly installed in their living room. Now, a decade and one half later, Buddy, with a permanent trailer hitched to his

Chrysler, carted the Hammond gig to gig. Never did learn how to read music.

During his teens, several of his friends on the street caught the motorcycle craze sweeping the Midwest, either tearing the bikes apart or rebuilding them in ramshackle garages behind their houses, then backfiring up and down DeForest Road late into the night. Buddy acquired an old jury-rigged Indian. Rupert and Myra, Buddy's mother, worried themselves sick about him damaging his piano hands. The clique grandstanded by riding the tracks down at the freight yard. The trick was to place a live motorcycle on a single track, then see how far and fast you could ride it before the bike veered off onto the ballast or cross ties. The neighbors began to bet money on the events. Buddy once kept the Indian on the polished rail clear up to Warren—a mile and a half north up the Mosquito Lake bed. By nighttime, however, you could hear him beating out the barrel-house tunes while Rupert and Myra rocked on the front porch swing, a thin wall away from their golden boy.

So there was no question that he was going to get out of East Niles and pull his family along with him. One day they would be listening to him over the airwaves. Might even see him in a picture show.

Perhaps that was the genesis of his obsession, reasoning it would be one thing if he stayed back in East Niles, married a neighbor girl, and got a job at Kennicut Copper like his father, a crane-handler, had. But Buddy Hart was destined for a house with plumbing, tailored suits, and a woman from Sandusky where all the wealth lay like some colossal liner, beguiling and luxurious. Well, perhaps that's why he began fixating about it.

Rupert couldn't quite believe the question.

"Are you shitting me?"

"I ain't."

"What's wrong with it? Looks fine to me."

"Yeah, maybe to you. But it's a stigma."

"What do you mean, *a stigma?*"

"A stain of disgrace, a tattoo or something that labels me a gully-jumper. Like somebody stamped me."

"Jesus Christ, Buddy . . . my old man, your uncles . . . nobody I've ever known done any different. If you got the cojones to ask your mother—and she can find it in her soul to be frank with you—well, *this is a damn happy family, boy!* Until now maybe. You thinking maybe we should have done something different?"

"I'm saying I don't want to go out there into the world smelling of DeForest Road. I won't have the mark of East Jesus on my forehead."

"Forehead!"

"Well, you know what I mean."

Rupert pulled out a cigarette. Buddy lit it for him. "What do you plan on doing about it now, Son?"

"Going to talk to Doc Green . . . tomorrow."

"Let me ask you something." Rupe's face flushed. "Did Wylie's daughter say something to you?" (Edgar Wylie, father of Buddy's current flame, owned the Pontiac dealership in Warren, and they did reside in Sandusky.)

"She has no idea."

"Don't bullshit me now. I'm your father—but we're men before we're anything else, remember, Buddy."

"My word."

"Is she why you're thinking about doing this?"

"Like I said, Buddy Hart's leaving Whistle Stop, clean. *I don't want to be marked.*"

\* \* \*

Doc Green's office was situated above a convenience store in the one-block commercial section of East Niles. Shine's Tavern, Tip-Top Bakery outlet and a beauty salon tucked in among several used car lots and auto repair shops. He treated his clientele like a cross between medical doctor and alcohol-on-the-breath priest. Doc tended to take no matter too seriously and did minor surgery in his office. Lilly, who had some nursing home experience, masked up

162 • OH, JOSEPHINE

for the occasions, while Green administered chloroform or ether to his trusting patients, many of whom kept a tab as sizable as the one they ran up on the grocery store's books. And when Buddy walked in, Green's eyes lit up.

"Bo Weevil, damn if you aren't one of the lucky ones!"

Buddy liked the Doctor's happy mien. "Howyadoin, Doc?"

"Getting your ass out of this crossroads. I don't expect to see you loitering out in front of Shine's, coming in here telling me you knocked up lissome Sarah Tisdale. 'Do you got any of them pills, Doc?' Or working over at Rank's bank, shining the ass on your gabardines like the rest of us mortals. Your poor old man's inhaled enough godforsaken sulfur over at the refinery for all of us. How is he, Buddy?"

"He's fine, Doc. Same as ever."

"And your Ma?"

"Still complaining . . . and washing cathouse laundry on weekends."

Doc Green winced. He'd been there in dual capacity.

"What can I do for you, son?"

Buddy got right to the issue, telling Doc Green how he thought it wasn't the fault of anybody. "The East-Jesus stigma . . . you know. Can you help me, Doc?"

Green got up, went to the cupboard, opened it, while Buddy surveyed the iodine-brown bottles with cork stoppers on the shelves. A veritable pharmacopeia. Green pulled one off the top shelf, placed two shot glasses on his desk. "Bourbon, son—the best. You going to another place, another country, stepping up to better circumstances, then you better learn the finest. *Salud*."

Buddy shivered as it rolled down his throat.

"I can perform the operation. We'll do it right here. Lilly Shine will have to assist. You don't mind her knowing, do you?"

"Is she a quiet one, Doc?"

"Lilly knows every damn secret in town." He chortled to himself. "She wouldn't even tell Al."

"How do I have to prepare?"

"Not a thing. Just haul your young ass in here next Tuesday at nine, I'll put you under, and you will be driving up DeForest Road by ten-thirty."

"Sounds like getting a tooth pulled, Doc."

"Decent analogy. Our father and uncles never knew any better."

"Do you mind my asking a personal question?"

"Shoot."

"How 'bout you?" Buddy gestured awkwardly. "Did you . . ."

The Doc smiled cagily. "Al Shine didn't put that peppermint glow on Lilly's face."

For the next several days it seemed everybody in Buddy's house spoke in riddles. He announced Doc Green was operating on him the following Tuesday, but nobody was sure why, except Rupert and his mother. And they were ashamed, if the truth be told. He hadn't intended it to be this way. But that's how it was turning out.

He told his girlfriend, Miss Wylie, he had to have a knee repaired. Fallen off the Indian a year back during one of those competitions. He'd be off his feet for a few days. Buddy's younger brother, Darius, had gone with him on his first visit to Dr. Green, sat in the car. Even during that trip back home, Buddy was elliptical.

"What's wrong with you, Buddy?"

"Ain't nothin' wrong with me . . . or you, for that matter. Can't really talk about it now. But I will someday when you're old enough."

"Why all the mystery, Buddy?" Darius had just turned fourteen.

"You know what goes on behind Rupe and Myra's door every night, Darius?"

"Nope."

"You can guess, though, huh?"

"Don't interest me enough."

"Like I said. Let's just say I'm getting my leg repaired."

"What's wrong with your leg, Buddy?"

"Bone has to be adjusted." Buddy turned the radio up loud. "Hello, Josephine" was playing.

Tuesday morning Darius asked to accompany Buddy to Doc Green's. Not wanting Rupert or Myra to accompany him, Buddy agreed. "It's a man's thing," he muttered. Again Darius waited in the Chrysler reading comic books. Buddy walked into Doc Green's office humming a tune, and less than an hour later strolled out . . . *"You used to use my umbrella every time it rained . . . and holler Woo woo woo."* He climbed into the car.

"Where are your crutches?" Darius asked.

"Crutches?"

"You know, for your leg."

Buddy laughed and pressed his foot on the starter. "Don't feel a thing."

"What happened?"

"Lilly Shine was suited up like in a white beauty-parlor costume wearing a mask and rubber gloves, and Doc had this barber's jacket on and wearing gloves, too. Took me into a white closet next to his smokey office, laid me on what looked like one of your library tables at school, tucked a souvenir cushion under my head—Niagara Falls—then Lilly slipped my trousers off."

"Yeah?"

"'You won't feel a thing,' Doc said, and put this rubber mask over my face. It had an air-pump hose connected to some green cylinders and smelled like strong cleaning solution to me, stronger than what Mama uses at the notcheries, and the next thing I knew—I was riding my Indian down the Chesapeake line on a sunny day. Sunlight glancing off the polished rail damn near blinded me. I was having trouble keeping the motorcycle balanced, feeling like I was going to tumble off . . . but instead of falling headfirst onto the cross ties, it was like I was going to fall into eternity . . . just blue sky with no clouds, no earth. Scary . . . but dreamy, too."

"Jesus. Did you feel any pain? Did they have knives and things out on the table?"

"No pain. None at all. And the knives I never saw. But he took Jack Perkins's leg off in that very same room a few years back when Jack fell drunk on the tracks and the 10:08 to Ashtabula didn't do the job completely. Lot of cuttin' has gone on in there. But, shit, Darius, I don't feel a damn thing." Buddy turned onto DeForest. *"Hello, Josephine. How do you do? Do you remember me, baby, like I remember you?"*

"Is your leg bandaged up?"

"Oh it's bandaged up all right."

"Can I see it?"

"When it's healed, I'll show you. Not before." The brothers remained stone silent the remainder of the fifteen minute trip.

In the driveway, Myra waited alongside her neighbors, Genevieve Glaxson and her married daughter, Nell. Buddy stepped out of the car like nothing happened.

"Did you go?" Myra asked, astonished.

"Yeah, he went," Darius answered.

"Well, did Doc Green do anything?"

Buddy smiled, put his arm around his mother's shoulder. "Did it all, Ma. East Niles is back in sawbones' waste can. But I'm hungry as a horse."

Myra gestured to the two women she'd meet up with them later, and, bemused, walked into the kitchen behind Buddy. He asked for scrambled eggs and bacon. "While you're gettin' it ready, Ma, I'm just going in here to lie down for a bit." Buddy poured himself a cup of coffee and went into the living room. Darius followed and sat at his brother's feet on the end of the sofa. Hardly five minutes passed before Darius could see Buddy begin to sweat heavily.

"You all right, Buddy?"

"Yeah . . . yeah, I'm all right."

Buddy began to unbutton his trousers.

"You gonna show me the operation, Buddy?"

Buddy had begun to groan and wasn't speaking now . . . ever so cautiously easing his trousers off his hips. Darius moved closer. *"Oh, for Chrissake! Please don't move. Don't move the fucking sofa . . . MA!"*

Myra rushed into the room. Buddy jerked board-stiff, his back arched and his legs out before him on the sofa, his pants down to his knees . . . still wearing Y fronts. Darius and she saw it seeping through his crotch. A circle about the size of an eye—and growing.

"Help me, OH GOD . . . HELP ME! GET MY TRUNKS OFF ME. MA! Cut them away from me. *Jesus Christ, I'm dying!*"

Darius and Myra eased Buddy onto the living room floor and Myra removed his shoes, sliding his trousers off him. Buddy hammered his fists against the floor, crying for her to drop his trunks. Darius could see nothing wrong with his legs. Myra rushed out of the room and returned with her pinking shears, snipping the jockey shorts in two at his hip, tenderly peeling them off his genitalia. Buddy's swathed member oozed crimson.

*"MA. Do something. Get me ice, put a fan on it!"*

Darius fetched ice and Myra placed a cold compress to her son's head.

Rupert appeared in the doorway. "Doc Green told us to expect this," he drawled, and sat on the sofa watching his eldest writhe and groan on the floral carpet. "Exactly like he said—*'The boy's gonna step out of his car like a cock of the walk, Rupe . . . but in minutes he'll be parading the East Jesus's secret to the world. It's just gonna take time. Let him drink whiskey and thump on the walls.*

*"'Ain't natural for a man to get that operation twenty years after the fact. God bless him. But in one week he'll look like all the other pricks in Sandusky County.'"*

# ACKNOWLEDGMENTS

Many of the stories in this collection appeared in the following publications:

Alsop Review, "Banjo Grease," "Chrysalis," "Cloth," "Escape," "Horace," "Passing Through Ambridge," "Popeye's Dead," "Say Hello to Stanley," "The Scar"; American Jones Building & Maintenance, "White Shoulders"; ATOM MIND, "Passing Through Ambridge," "Popeye's Dead"; Best of the Year, CrossConnect Anthology, "Big Whitey"; Blue Cathedral: Short Fiction for the New Millennium, "Say Hello to Stanley"; Blue Moon Review, "Oh, Josephine"; CrossConnect, "Big Whitey"; FUEL Magazine, "Oh, Josephine"; Fiction 2000, "Say Hello to Stanley"; Java Snob Review, "Passing Through Ambridge"; Lynx Eye, "Say Hello to Stanley"; Oval Magazine, "Popeye's Dead"; Pangolin Papers, "Day Laborer"; Porcupine Literary Arts Magazine, "Banjo Grease"; Red Rock Review, "Escape"; Rosebud, "The Pruner"; Salt Hill Journal, "Chrysalis"; Southern Indiana Review, "The Scar"; Sou'wester, "Escape"; Sundog, the Southeast Review, "Banjo Grease"; Talus and Scree International Journal, "Big Whitey"; Taproot Literary Journal, "Horace"; Writer's Forum, "Escape"; and Yefief, "Cloth."

"Say Hello to Stanley" won First Prize in the Alsop Review in 1999. "Horace" won First Prize in Taproot Literary Journal's National Competition in 1998. "Popeye's Dead" won First Prize in the Oval Magazine's National Competition in 1996.

## BIOGRAPHICAL NOTE

Dennis Must is the author of three novels: *Brother Carnival* (Red Hen Press, November 2018), *The World's Smallest Bible* (Red Hen Press, March 2014), and *Hush Now, Don't Explain* (Coffeetown Press, October 2014), as well as three short story collections: *Going Dark* (Coffeetown Press, 2016), *Oh, Don't Ask Why* (Red Hen Press, 2007), and *Banjo Grease* (Creative Arts Book Company, 2000). He won the 2014 Dactyl Foundation Literary Fiction Award for *Hush Now, Don't Explain*, and *The World's Smallest Bible* was a 2014 USA Best Book Award Finalist in the Literary Fiction category. His plays have been produced Off-Off Broadway and he has been published in numerous anthologies and literary journals. He resides with his wife in Salem, Massachusetts.